Published by: Desmond Denton, Cape Town, South Africa
Interior Design by: Jessica Sprong, Creative Junkie Studio
Cover Design by: Jessica Sprong, Creative Junkie Studio

A DESMOND DENTON STORY
SPELONK
A WORLD UNDONE
CHRISTINE
TESCO
ERIC
UYS
GREG
KRIEK
ABDURAGMAN
ADAMS
FALLOUT SHELTER AHEAD
CAPE TOWN

A SPECIAL THANK YOU

One of the most important elements of being in the film and TV industry is understanding the value of team and networking.

Having a team of passionate filmmakers can bring the black and white text of a script into a magical story.

Special thanks to all the crew, cast and sponsors involved in creation of the film.

Special credit to the assistant writers and editors:
Edward Bennett, Tamzin Atkins, Shervaan Baros and David Barbier.

On behalf of the entire production team, we would like to thank all our contributors for their generous support and for making this dream a reality.

We want to urge everyone visiting the site **www.spelonkfilm.**com to take a moment and help support the companies involved

FUTURE CAPE TOWN

Clearly, humans are a force of nature, but unlike any other natural disaster, we are not only the cause of so much destruction, we participate in it.

The film in itself is an act of awareness, of our impact on nature, each other and bringing about the question of what future are we shaping, or passively watching as it is shaped by others.

The film brings about the best of an post apocalyptic action film with a tale of caution to society, a testament to people who care about future generations.

ONCE UPON A TIME...

There was a boy who was inspired by telling stories. He lost himself in books so much that he had to start telling the stories with friends via a video tape recorder. He and his friends used to cut together their own movies and handmade title sequences.

He would wake up to see a world filled with drama, conflict, suspense, adventure, and fantasy. It made him feel alive. He would just sit and listen to people and came to this amazing conclusion…

People are moved by emotion and the best emotions are usually engaged by this simple phrase…*once upon a time…*

He believed that one needs to be training your mind as well as skill. So what did he do next? He started in school working on film sets, from being a runner, making coffee and getting to know the film hierarchy. He studied, worked hard and fell more in love with the film industry. So the next best thing to do was to enroll to the Afda film school where he studied directing and writing.

Over the years he had the priviledge to work on national and international films and with filmmakers. One of his biggest tests was to take on the 48hour film challenge. It went great! He and his team got 12 nominations and 3 awards.

He has been involved in filmmaking in various ways and represents international films through cinema in South Africa.

He and his brother, Marinus started their own production company Imagenheart and quickly became very productive with big name clients.

Because of his love to do pitching, do visual research and finding ways to creatively tell stories, it brought together a unique combination of skills from pre-production to the end product. He would enjoy the challenge of pitches and over the years had successfully pitched and launched various commercials for clients, secured sponsors for films and distribution.

The boy with dreams, is now an award winning filmmaker who walks with a strong vision of creativity, vision, passion and heart. This fearless and talented man is...

DESMOND DENTON
International award winning storyteller

HOW IT ALL STARTED...

Spelonk have been inspired by a big love for history, folklore, creating South African films that can bridge our borders...all these elements and yet one key component has been driving it all along.

A large part of writing Spelonk came from having my first daughter, Katelyn. It has been an incredible journey this far and I feel like I am learning so much about myself, the world world and finding big truths with her in the middle of ordinary moments. I have been fortunate to travel with her to countries such as USA and, Istanbul and first hand experience how the world came alive to her. As I am a writer, director and storyteller, I ask myself what story do I tell little Katelyn about the world she grows up in. What hope do I grow in her heart?

Spelonk has become my personal question - what world little Katelyn will grow up in, what world we leave behind. It is a journey of hope and yet sometimes fear.

Dealing within a context of South Africa where there is a strong dual view - Firstly looking at the country with what it has accomplished, the rainbow nation, filled with potential, talent, creativity, with hope. A place where people have found ways to get together beyond our differences, to build a new nation. I grew up seeing the miracle, the change of Apartheid to the rainbow nation and stood up together as we triumphed over many obstacles.

One can't ignore the current reality which often overshadows this hope. While many emigrate away whether due to economical or safety reasons - I believe we should look at both sides of the coin. In this country of hope, I often find myself in thought regarding what we can do to change the situation. The rainbow nation becomes a chess board of black and white, and the rainbow nation magic seems to fade. All this happens while top level politicians often merely laugh when addressed about matters of importance.

Clearly, humans are a force of nature, but unlike any other natural disaster, we're not only the cause of destruction, we participate in it (whether directly involved, or passively watching).

The film in itself is an act of awareness, question of what future are we shaping, or passively watching as it is shaped by others.

Our apocalypse is not caused by the *what if*
It is caused by the *what if we don't*

1

For the Angel of Death
spread his wings on the blast,
And breathed in the face
of the foe as he passed;
And the eyes of the sleepers
waxed deadly and chill,
And their hearts but once heaved,
and forever grew still!

Lord Byron

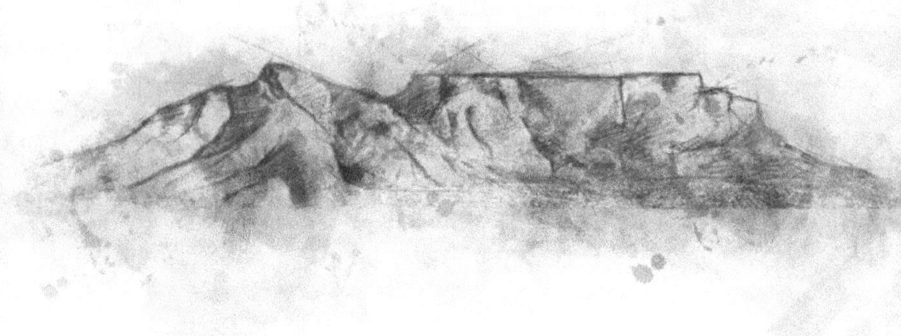

A silent dusty road, once a lush landscape of beauty and reverence… Now it's a desert land of waste, nothing but decay, death its closest friend. The only sound in the distance coming from an old Royal Enfield motorbike... The sound of the motor the loud metallic hum of its roaring engine, breaking the all but silent atmosphere... The figure on it, a legend at most and myth to others, cloaked from head to toe. No one knows how He looks until death creeps from his hands, blink and you'll miss his steely gaze, all that is known of him is the dark red colored stains on his cloak. He doesn't creep in the shadows; he is the shadows himself! A man that carries what many want. Many would kill for, and many would die for it. The Rider is confident, even with one robotic arm. The bike suddenly jerks a few times. The rider tries to keep it steady as it suddenly cuts out. He looks around the deserted road and gets off the bike. No fuel, a scarce resource like most in these times. The sword attached to his side, a reminder of who he was. Not just a bounty hunter, he carries himself with the poise of highly trained Military Elites. A man known only as Dante, he knew nothing but violence, every footstep he took would be stained with blood of anyone whoever dared stand in his way. They say that men who walk in solitude across the desert are in search of one of two things: purpose, or death. Dante thought to himself:" would my death be at the hands of nature, or some fool who got lucky?" He trails his hands through the course, sun-bleached sand. He had a mission to complete, a promise made on death row. Not even Mother Nature herself would hinder this quest. She had played her hand already. Now it was his turn!

He had felt like he had walked this path many times and it sometimes felt pointless. Looking for a ghost of a man, he was looking for any sign that he was real. They were two men from opposing worlds, specters to the outside world. His feet carrying him against his will away from his beloved motorbike, towards the endless sandy dunes. A veil of sand streamed across his vision, it would strip a man of his skin if given the chance."What a place to break down" Dante thought. The sand so deep, it came up to his ankles, he could feel the heat through his boots. This was No Man's Land, a land of thirst and hunger. His thirst became unbearable. He tears off a button from his coat and sucks on it in hopes of producing saliva, as he had nothing but empty canisters on him. If he were to die here, at least his grave would bury him. A hero's death, all but a myth... Across from him like a mirage, a traffic light is wedged in the sand. Reminiscent of a life once lived by scores of people. Where cars drove freely and trees grew along the sides of walkways with kids running along them, kites and dogs to follow. An ancient dream of normalcy, a world where you were free to be human and not be a monster to survive... Then he sees it, a movement in the distance. Was it real or something he wanted to see? Dante walks closer, clenching his robotic hand as a reminder of what he has lost. The sun strokes his face, revealing signs of countless battles.

The man lies tied to a pole with barbed wire, a death trap for many. His eyes look vacant, every breath almost his last as the wire cuts deeper. Dante looks down at the pitiful site and wishes that he saw more than a meal for someone else. Wishes he saw a human and not just another failure in this thing called life. He wonders what she would think, what she would do if she saw this man. Dante would not go there, those thoughts led to destruction. He could not afford to feel anything. He knelt down on one knee, a bag of treasures lying just out of the man's reach. Dante opens it, hoping to find anything of worth. He looks at the man, not a word coming from his sun-dried lips. Dante pulls out pieces of various electronic devices, parts that were useless to anyone but scavengers. He throws them aside and finds something worthwhile. A can of old beans, the tin rusted and dirty, but the lure of something to drink enough for him to take it. Dante turns back to the man, who was still not even registering that Dante was even there. Dante takes his elite force watch out from the front pouch of his old worn backpack and flips open the cover to reveal the very person Dante was in search of. He shows it to his fellow companion in this dying world of flies eating live carcasses just to survive.

"Seen him?" holding up the wanted poster of a man.

The man's eyes flicked for a second before staring out into the vast expanse of nothing. No answer, he was too far gone. Dante stands up and takes out an old knife and drops it by the man out of pity. Hoping that one day if he was ever in this situation, karma would come find him.

Dante walked on, holding the can in his hand, he looked down at it and took out a knife, stabbing the top with the force of a starving man. The opening of the can greeted Dante with a stinging waft that over stayed its welcome. The beans have aged, like flies' white pin-needle eggs that brood in swashing liquid. Mold gathered like thick greenish-gray webs around the can's edges. Despite the smell the liquid was a goddess' gift. Without a second's doubt desperation took over and he lugged down the particle infested water. It wasn't much, but he lived with it. Choking it down without stopping for breath...”You gotta do what you gotta do” he thought, tightening the muscles in his neck to keep himself from retching. No time to think. The reaction was instant. The rancid beans began eating him up inside, tiny nails of worms piercing through his guts. Reality began skipping a frame, the first sign of losing one's sanity. His steps felt floaty, a false euphoria poured into his soul and for once it stared him in the eye. He fell to his knees, the world amiss around him. Familiar voices... A touch of tender hands, that once saw the war yet were still just as soft.

They touched him with a feeling that made him think maybe if he had a mother she would have touched him like that. Who was she? Why was she so familiar? Why did he feel pain at the mere thought of her? Her face was blurry, a mirage of pain and blackened whispers. A smile that melted the strongest of hearts and yet he couldn't quite place her. It was hard for him to comprehend that she could in such little time change all he knew… his former life… his way of being.

2

"Before the
Earth choked"

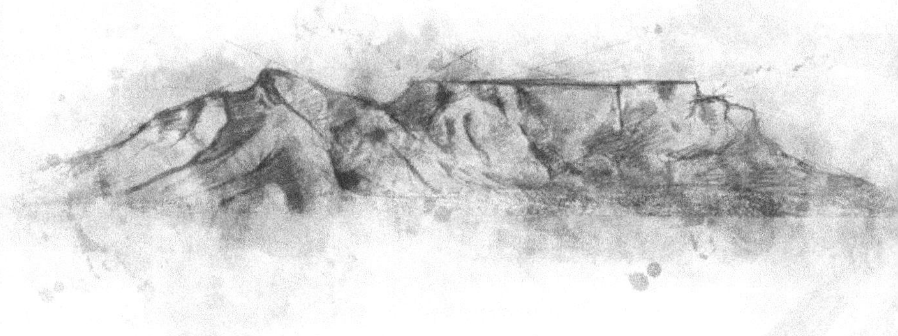

The aroma in the air was rancid, like charred ash and rotting flesh. This was home, a place where many lived. A place where many died every hour... The general population dwindling every second as someone was murdered over a sip of clean water. She stood on top of the pile of dilapidated cars, looking out at her community. It was one of the better places she had lived. It had broken down structures that people had claimed as homes and a sense of community. The people here cared for each other. The Commando Rebels camped in the outpost. Out of reach from the military... Ended up in nothing but an old town, a dust heap of broken dreams as they try to rebuild what is left of society.

The woman standing above all with a sense of dread in her gut was called Ophelia. For some she was a rebel, but to others a savior. She was fierce as ever, with the will to survive, a trait many had lost. She jumped down and walked towards her leader and close friend, Emile, if anyone had those anymore. Emile was cloaked head to toe; the dust would destroy his lungs otherwise. He had on a one of a kind navy blue jacket and the common rebel leather masks and wrist bands. His boots had walked miles, holes in the heels would be plugged with anything that would stick, long term temporary fixes. He looked to be in a fierce discussion with Nantes, a guy who was the Keeper of Water. The man was flailing his arms around as he spoke. Ophelia approached.

"What's the problem here Gents?" asks Ophelia. Emile turns and looks at Ophelia, she was beautiful to him, with ivory skin and long black hair, a rare attribute in this harsh landscape. But she was also a strong warrior and fierce fighter. She walked like a goddess, with the elegance only a lady in the 19th century bore. She would lure you in with her smile, and kill you with the ferocious tenacity of a Black Widow.

"We're low on water." answers Nantes. He was a small old man and most importantly Emile's only living relative. Family was scarce, not everyone survived. But Nantes was strong and he knew everything going on.

"But we got two loads last week!" Ophelia cries.

"The community is growing larger; we need more water to survive." says Emile "We can't keep doing this, it's dangerous and it doesn't feel right." replies Ophelia. "We have no choice!" yells Emile.

"I will leave you two to chat, remember the season is changing, the soil is ruined by ash and blight. To survive we need to do what is wrong with what is right as the end goal." states Nantes as he leavpes.

Ophelia cross her arms and stand facing Emile. "I can't keep doing this."

"It is for the good of the people." answers Emile.

"I am the one putting my life in danger and it is getting harder."

"Please we need you."

Suddenly a young dirty boy, with scraps for clothing and skin caked in filth calls out to them."It's happening; Miss June is havin' the baby." He stares at Ophelia and Emile, lasting a second. A desperate, pleading look radiating from his face...

"I'm coming, where is she?" asks Ophelia turning away from Emile.

Night fell and Miss June was covered in sweat and grime, she lay with her legs wide open and screamed so loudly it echoed all the way through the encampment.

"It's okay, just take a deep breath" says Galio the community doctor, a man in his late fifties who was once known as a nurse back in his day.

"No it won't be okay, get this thing out of me."

"It is going to be your child, June. No matter who is responsible, you will look at this baby and love it because it is a part of you." pleads Ophelia.

"And a part of him..." Spat June.

"I need you to give me one last push, I see the head." "Please get me some water." calls Ophelia holding Junes hand.

This was no place for a baby to be born, in a dirty place like this.

The walls were crumbling and they had a small bit of candlewax to light the room. June had on a once white dress that was large on her sickly thin frame. Even with her pregnant belly she was thinner than usual." Miss Ophelia there's no water left." says the boy. He was an apprentice for the doctor, no more than twelve but took death in a stride and blood as water to the thirsty.

"Please just cut it out" screams June," I don't want to do this anymore!" Her eyes were glossy and she looked pale. The floor was covered in blood, the puddle growing rapidly. The doctor calls Ophelia aside.

"If she doesn't push now they both will die." Ophelia looks down at the woman and takes a deep breath. She walks up to the woman and kneels down till she's looking the woman in the eye.

"This baby is coming whether you like it or not. So either help us get it out sooner or suffer and you both die."

June contemplates her choice and with one last scream pushes with all her might. The room filled with a deathly silence as the young apprentice cut the cord. The baby was small. A little girl with thick black hair, ten fingers and ten toes… But no sound was emitting from her tiny mouth. Ophelia steps closer as the doctor attempts to make her breathe.

"What's wrong, give it to me" cries June.

"She not breathing." whispered the boy.

"I don't feel well" mumbled June her eyes rolling back and her body convulsing, her skin turning pale, her lips blue.

Ophelia's handed the limp baby as the doctor and his apprentice run over to help June. Ophelia looks down at the baby still covered in amniotic fluid.

"Come on little girl, I know this world isn't great but we need you to live." Says Ophelia massaging on the baby's chest. The commotion around her dies out as she focuses all of her attention on the little bundle in her arms. Suddenly the baby's hand twitches and a wail erupts from the beautiful pouty lips of the newborn babe. Ophelia smiles and turns around, only to stop suddenly at the site of the doctor and his apprentice covering June's body up in a blanket. Stunned, Ophelia's eyes drift down to the screaming baby and back at the woman. A tear leaks out to glide down her cheek and onto the baby. This is the life she was living, one where death was your partner, ever faithful in its duties. She blindly hands the baby over to the young boy and stumble out of the room. Ophelia feels cold, her arms wrap tightly around her waist. She tries to scream, but her breath pulls back.

It was dark, not a single star in the inky black sky. The screaming sound of the baby could still be heard, echoing in her mind. Ophelia hears the crunch of heavy footsteps in the dry sand and deep breathing. Emile follows dragging in a man, dressed in fine clothing. Unlike any Ophelia has seen before. His body is scarred, blistered by the desert sun. He mumbles under his breath. The man stares up into the dark space and reaches out with his broken and mangled hands. Emile brings over an antiquated electronic device to scan the man for his identity.

"Who is this man?" whispers Ophelia.

"The answer to our prayers…" Emile mutters.

"I don't understand how he can be the answer?"

"He's got credit, a lot of it and with credit, we can again get water without getting noticed." explained Emile.

"I can't go through this again, people aren't currency Emile! It won't be long before they catch us or even worse, follow us back here!" shouts Ophelia.

"We don't have much of a choice. The men are out daily searching, testing, and trying. This man is dying, blind like a mole. Whoever he was, his days are counted. Please Ophelia, just this one time. Then we can move… We'll have enough water to head north to search further." says Emile.

Ophelia knew the procedure by now. It was a painful process, cutting out the electronic chip from the man's hand, and carefully planting it into her hand. Ophelia leans back, cringing from the pain as they inject it between the veins, careful not to make the scar too obvious. This time would be her last she promises herself, there had to be another way. This was not the time for philosophy or long discussions. Times were desperate. It wasn't about her convictions, but the livelihood of everyone she knew. It was hard to even think of the world as it was before. The vision becomes dimmer as time goes by. Pictures and sounds of better times…

We were careless back then, with everything. The irony was now it seems the earth under our feet paid back our callous attitudes in kind. It's been a long while since there has been any fresh rain. Acid water has drenched the earth, destroying what little green tried to sprout. The smell, the stench of decay and desperation would be the hands about our collective throat.

The group left at dawn, Ophelia was wrapped in a shawl with her arm healing fast. The implant a constant reminder of what was about to happen. A shiver like ice runs down her spine. Emile walks ahead of them, keeping a clear look out as they make their way towards the Water-Station. They need to be careful. The open road's not a place to be caught off guard. Here, toll-payment was due in blood by way of murder, or worse. The road was marked by dried husks of once men, those who have not made it to the Water-Station, others those who fought and rose up as a rebellion against the military. The Commando Rebels have grown over the years, but after the failed rebellion they split into scattered groups for a chance to survive. The remnant now fights a Guerrilla War against the plutocracy.

Only the strongest and smartest were chosen for this mission. Never using the same people, always new ones, except for Ophelia... She has been to the Water-Station a few times, constantly changing her look, her walk, her being. This time though Ophelia was restless. This life was daunting at most.

It took hours for them to get there, their feet covered in sores, shoes worn. Walking in such a way to ensure that people can't track them back to their camp... The Rebels are wanted by the military. Even though their numbers are inferior they have been able to create massive tension for the military leaders, being able to steal water resources, weaponry as well as various ambush situations. The Water-Station known as the Tannery, has a legendary history of being one of the oldest and biggest tanneries in the country. This factory stood for over 200 years but with the fall, very little remained of formal society and economy. Theft soon led to the barred building becoming nothing more than a ruin of the past.

Within a few years, the military needed a refinery, for water purification. This big building became a good outpost. Water runs from a deep underground source, yet it needs to be purified. The water used to keep the machines running, is then allocated for use by the 'common' people, as they say. Even the brown, greasy water was a precious resource to the desperate. The Military knew that they would be able to retain their power in the smaller towns outside Cape Town by controlling the water. With this they were able to keep a strange sense of order. People worked in groups, small communities that were able to trade their time and other resources for water. Those who refused had to find other ways to means of water, for which little was known. In the towns theft and crime was not tolerated and the military would set an example of those who moved beyond their set out rules. People scattered across the dried-out lands in search of other means. Most never to be seen again... The Tannery had a strange smell when one came close to the building, that of old rotten leather. In the colder winter months, when the acid water would fill the old tanks, the stench of the left-over leather deposits could be smelt miles away.

The military didn't do much to keep this old ruin in good shape. It was guarded and barbed-wire fencing was put up, with many parts of the building in a dangerous state. Those who dared to get to the water machinery often felt trapped, either by the guards or by the decaying building itself. The bricks had become brittle over the long period of time without up-keep. Dried weeds still fastened like veins to the outer walls. Where it broke apart, small spots of light shone through onto the cold cement floors. Now it was little more than a tool in the hands of power.

"People are cattle" thought Dante, as he watched from above the Water-Station. The Elite Force troops were on a tracking mission, they set out to find a specific leader from the rebel group. The Water-Station was the starting point for their investigation as it had people gathering from all around. They were easily herded without even realizing it. When it comes to things in their best interest, they will stubbornly burn bridges. Yet they welcome destruction without a second thought. No, people are not cattle, they're forms of credit, and they are expendable. To Dante it was a straight forward mission. One of many he has taken on through the years. There has not been any significant resistance, towns were burnt to the ground where people did try and defy them.

Times were desperate and without a sense of order, there would be no hope, or so they were told.

***

Driven by some latent instinct, they swerve and rise without even truly knowing why. Their chants fuel the rhythm of their stampede. Soldiers hopelessly try to hold back the onslaught of the crowd. When you first join the Cape Frontier, you think you'll be helping people, not herding them. Today these young soldiers learnt the truth of what it meant to be in the frontier military, you are at the frontier of human madness. The lower minorities push forward, fighting to get to the water housed in the factory, violently thirsty. A couple of days ago, a battalion of Frontier troops set up camp and locked this place down. The Intel painted this water plant as feeding the rebellion rats that move along the industrial wasteland borders nearby. Closing the plant down meant that nobody got water, except for the Cape Frontier. This lockdown pissed the locals off who depended on the plant for its drips of water, some of them even worked inside. And here they were dealing with this volcanic situation. Here Dante was in the middle of it again. They chant biting words, one mouth utters,"You evil bastards. Corrupt Devils from Hell! Can't you see we are dying. When we die, you'll starve!"

"Yes, we are corrupt and you are not my people" thought Dante. Dying was their problem. Pick up a gun and do something about it. The mass of bodies scrum against the factory gate, skin shifting through the mesh while it rattles a Christmas jingle. Rock mortars are launched from the distances and shower down on the young soldiers. A hail of stones... Ophelia joined the line as others also slotted in, with even more people begging on the side. She stood watching people get rejected and leave with no water. The line took most of the day, guards with guns standing all around. Barbed wire fencing and scanners are used to keep the unwanted out. A young girl, dirty and alone made her way towards the line. Ophelia looked back once more at the rest of her crew hidden amongst the people in line. Third from the front, she wants to scratch at the electronic chip but holds back the urge. The man in front walks away with one bottle of water. The next woman in line has two children, a girl and a sick looking boy. The guard scans her and shakes his head. The boy coughs as the little girl starts crying.

"Please sir, my boy is really sick. Just a little bit." pleads the mother.

"Hendriks." calls the Guard.

———

The woman and her children are ushered out by the guard named Hendricks. The woman tries to resist but the gun against her back cuts down any odds of her being successful. The place is filling up around them. Cyborgs are seen chatting in groups, a bottle of water amongst them. Ophelia steps forward, holding her hand out.

"I want to withdraw… All of it." She says.

———

The guard scans her wrist; Ophelia makes eye contact with Emile who nods in approval. Emile stands on the side, pretending to be a beggar, asking for water from those who exit the line. His face covered by filth and a torn cowl, his eyes black, staring back at her. The guard brings a trolley forward with bottles of water. The guard hesitates for a moment, holding the cart firmly with one hand. He looks at Ophelia with skepticism.

"Let me scan again." demands the guard.

Ophelia nods and hands him her wrist, he scans it.

"Something wrong?" asks Ophelia.

"Double Procedure, we have had some system errors lately" answers the guard. After a few tense seconds the Guard looks over at his partner and calls him. "Hendriks!"

Ophelia knows that tone of voice.

"I don't understand. I know I have credit left, I worked for these."

The guard looks at the screen flickering and sees the credits on the system. It was clear there was more going on here than meets the eye. Ophelia cringes as she feels the gun pushing against her back. All this effort was for nothing. She knew she couldn't leave empty handed."I'm certain sir, check again." Ophelia said as she is slowly pushed away.

Hendriks is moving Ophelia away from the line, but in a different direction than the ones leaving the building. Emile knew there was trouble. He pushes through the gathering crowd towards Ophelia, struggling to get his gun. He nears the guard escorting Ophelia, and without hesitation kicks the guard in the back so hard the leather clad man falls to the ground.

This was just the moment the enraged people were waiting for, breakdown of civil order. Chaos erupts as people in line moved out, forcefully making their way towards the water reserves. The rebels overpower the guards quickly, with only minor casualties on their side at first. Some of the guards break their line, running away from the enraged horde of people. They manage to get a distress call through to their HQ. Soon enough the crowd turns on each other for the water. They tear each other apart clawing at bottles of the pure liquid. Guards who weren't quick enough were trampled to death along with civilian stragglers. Weapons taken at the entrance was retrieved, all kinds - from spanners and rusty blades to guns still holstered on the dead guards. The crowd soon overpowers their wardens, taking control and seizing the reserve. Blood splattered the dusty floors and walls, flowing down the old rusted drainpipes, thinned out by mass amounts of spilt water.

Ophelia watches in horror. The scene an echo of"Dull Gret" by Pieter Bruegel... Chaos and confusion. This wasn't her intention. A simple mission to retrieve water to give to her people, to move North. Emile and the other rebels took the situation as an opportunity. While people were crazily grabbing for water, they were taking water and moving it outside, getting much more than they could carry. Emile sent them in pairs out to take water back to their camp. He and Ophelia would be the last to leave.

The adrenaline was still high, the crowd had already changed, some new faces made their way inside, having heard about the water situation. Suddenly heavily armed military forces were moving in, having rappelled down from the open building top. A cyborg guarding the premises is shot through the head instantly as well as another Rebel on watch. Dante, followed by his unit breaks into the Water-Station, running down the staircase in the center of the building. As Dante steps onto the floor, he shoots an armed man a short distance away. Emile hears the shot. Running towards it, he sees Dante. Emile attempts to sneak up behind Dante, brandishing a large knife to finish him quietly. But Dante turns around instinctively and shoots Emile in the gut. He falls to the floor, his hands trying to stop the blood flowing freely from his stomach.

It was a matter of moments before the military took back the space. One of the Elite Force soldiers shouts loudly, demanding everyone to lie flat on the floor. Some ignore him, trying to make their way to the exit with water and are shot down without hesitation. The more compliant people are held at gunpoint as the military men move between them, lying between the muddy mix of blood and water, situated between the dead and wounded.

Dante walks up to a guard who is badly wounded. He spots Ophelia from the corner of his eye, still standing. The heat that was the mob has suddenly cooled down until their wretched silence fills the old building. Everyone looks around at dead friends, dead enemies and dead people. Suddenly they feel the weight of the situation. They are still on edge but now too afraid to move, too afraid of this shadow. Entering the jittery crowd, Dante is greeted with eyes of fear. They know who he is and what he is capable of. Death himself rode behind his every step. Deep down, he prayed for one of the meek to spring forth and cut towards him. He hungered for a blood show.

"You!" shouts Dante.

He marches on Ophelia who stands proudly, wrapped in her shawl. Bennett, his leader and mentor fast approaching them.

"So you're the trouble maker." Affirms Dante.

"Acting against the Authorities is severely punishable, take it off." Bennett states.

Ophelia stare back at them, not an ounce of fear showing.

"We have the right to water, it belongs to everyone." Replies Ophelia.

In the corner of her eye she could see Emile lying there wounded and bleeding. She fears for him, but hides it under her strong demeanor.

"Take it off." order Dante.

He steps forward and pulls the shawl off revealing her arms.

"No marks or injections. Are you a Cape Rebel?" ask Dante.

Everyone who worked and stayed within the colony and settlements were marked by the military, she however had another sign, one that the military knew well, the sign of the Cape Rebels. The layers of clothing kept it hidden, but now little was to be revealed. Ophelia looks straight at Dante but says nothing. Her spirit wanting to fight back but she knows well that she is outnumbered and that if Emile would dare stand up he would most definitely be killed.

"Do you know what we do with *would be* heroes? Take her away." Dante said.

A guard grabs her arm and shoves his loaded rifle into her back, leading her away.

There was something different about this girl, her way of standing amidst the chaos. Dante noted it down on his comm-watch. They seem to become more defiant, even facing death openly. It was clear that the harsh treatment and warning of the military was not enough to defeat the human spirit. Dante knew that this girl's spirit will soon be broken once she is interrogated, tested and laid to as a subject for military scientists who saw little of the outside world except for the information they got from their test subjects.

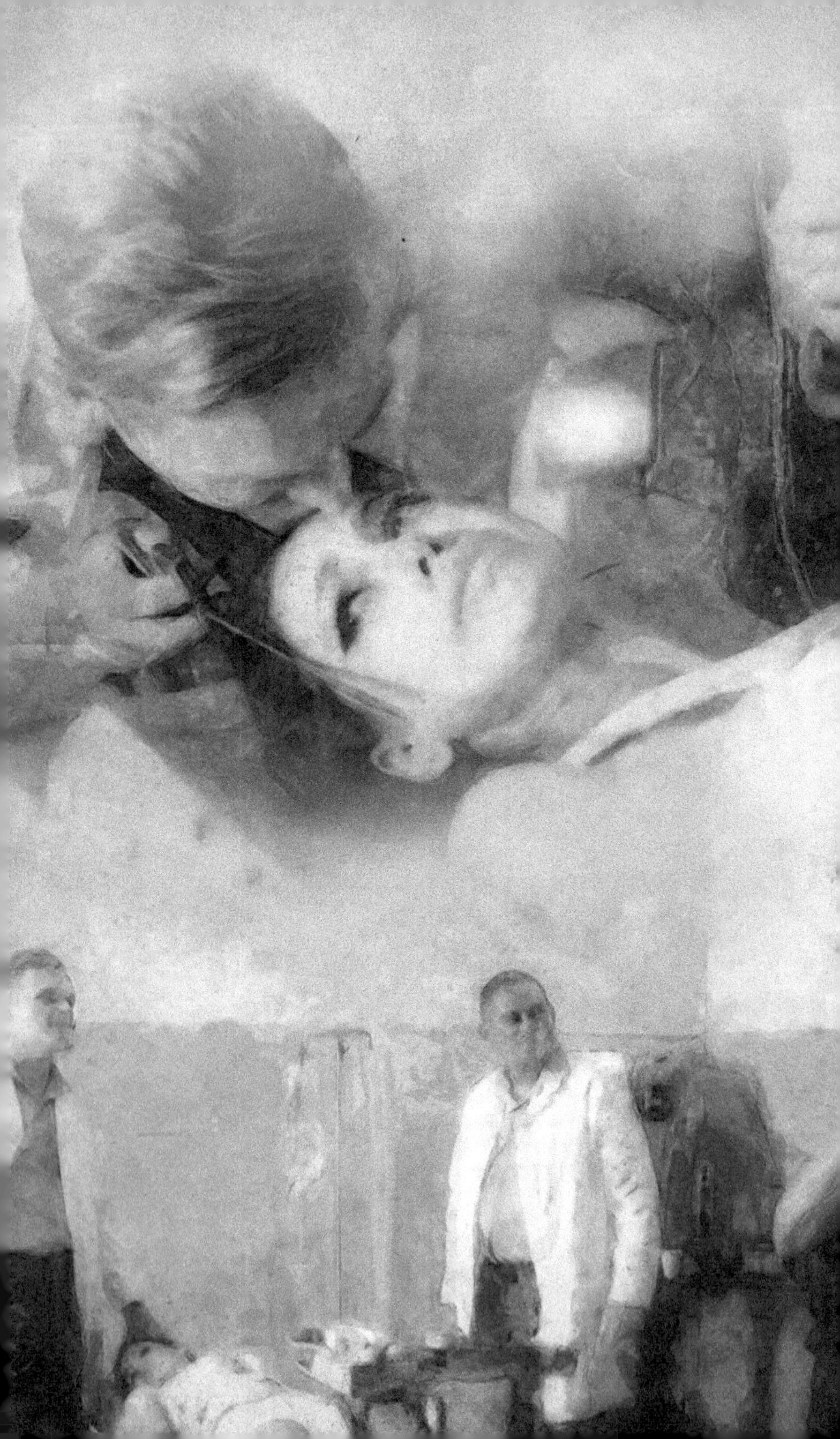

3

Chaos Reigns

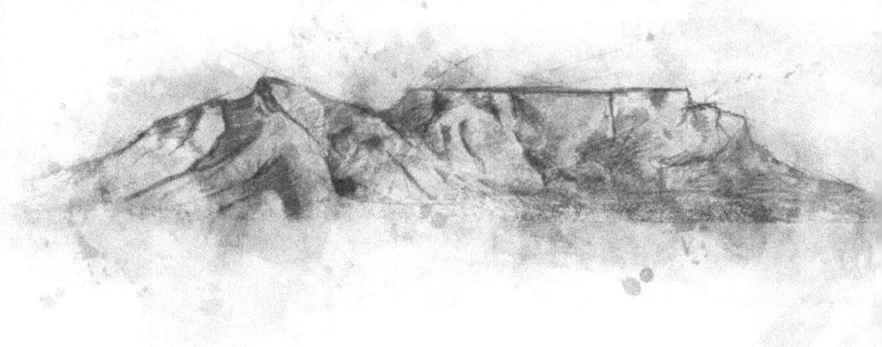

Dante woke up startled by nightmarish visions of the past. Fragments he wished he could bury. He looked around the room, inky blackness still enveloping it. Dante switched the lamp on and looked at his comm-watch. It was still in the early hours of the morning. He pushed the button to record a note.

"The disaster at the Water-Station was contained, casualties were high. One woman has taken a stand. She is a Rebel by nature and won't conform to our rules. I haven't seen such fight in someone in a really long time. I don't understand why they won't just obey. Why defy what little order we have in this world?"

He got out of bed and put on a pair of black military pants.

Dante left the room and made his way to the training room, sword in hand, a crucial part of his everyday routine. It has been a ritual ever since he was a very young boy. He knows very little of the world outside the military. They have been good to him, gave him a chance. He switched the lights on, embracing the room. He was the first here, as per norm. What else could be expected from a future commander? His track record of successful missions, recovering and tracking and his kill record was clear to the others. There were all different kinds of gym equipment made from whatever had been found. A scanner stood on the wall, keeping track of all who came. His comm-watch on his arm kept record of all his activities. Dante started off with the cold tub. His body was covered in scars from previous engagements. The aim activity was to expand lung capacity. Dante got into the cold icy water tub and kept his breath, the watch on his arm becomes blue, showing the time, his heartrate and air left in his system. Molecular tracking was a common practice in the military. Nano-cells were injected into them that could respond to their watches, carrying information, sometimes crucial for the survival of troops, or for research on those who have gone beyond the reach of military. The military was a combination of modern sciences and old military fighting. The watch becomes red: "Lung capacity exerted, O_2 at dangerous levels". Dante remains underneath the water, a sense of determination in him to stay under, to fight, even against himself. At last Dante breaks through the ice cold water gasping for air." New record" the watch responds." Advisement: High Levels of O_2 will eventually weaken lung capacity and vascular capabilities, do not attempt again." states the watch.

"Keep that off the record." he stated.

Dante called his personal trainer AI system Ragel, after his long-time childhood friend and fellow military trainee. Dante got up to stand under a heating system, his body adjusting to the new heat. His sword was never far from him. Light created beams as it shone through the acid clouds that moved over the scorched earth. Dante heard footsteps and reached for his blade. A familiar voice put him at ease. Her skin touches his arm. Dante's body is taught and sinewy from his years in the military, various scars cross over each other in thick gashes. Ragel stood there. Her feelings for him was clear, she took comfort, safety and a strange sense of love in him. For Dante, his focus has always been on the mission. Ragel was tall and thin with spikey blonde hair with a blue highlight. Her training made her almost as notorious as Dante himself. Many a man tried to take her down, even find their way in with her, but the stories of broken noses and ribs were known throughout. Only one man was ever able to really get close to her, and that was Dante.

"You up early again?" asked Ragel.

Dante just nodded and signaled into the room.

"Have we captured another one?" She asked.

Dante let's go of his sword and takes one of the wooden practice swords from the wall, standing with legs spread apart, ready to fight. Ragel knew Dante all too well, but even then it was difficult to out maneuver him. The sparring seems intensely intimate, like a dance. Dante never breaks his focus. His eyes glued to Ragel. The wooden blade hits her against the side of the head as she moves in, trying to land a hit. Ragel hardly had time to regain her composure before Dante kicks her as she lies on the floor. She rolls further away, quickly assessing where he is. She draws her tactical side blade. The game is on. Dante smirks slightly at the sight of the large blade she holds out, ready to draw blood. It's all in the eyes, learn to anticipate the move, don't strike where he is, strike where he is going, use the energy of your opponent. Ragel strikes towards Dante cutting into his black training pants. He pulls back, no blood lost. Ragel slices towards the training sword as Dante moves around her with catlike movements. He is in control, moving in a motion that is difficult to track. The fast strikes have both of them breathing hard, sweating in the heated space. The fighting becomes more intense. Dante keeps low, going under Ragel's strikes. He leans back far, kicking up into Ragel's chest, launching her back at least by a meter. Shouts echo between blows. Fatigue takes the bench as adrenaline takes the wheel. Ragel is ferocious. Her close quarters fighting style reminiscent of Krav Maga. She manages to down Dante with an elbow to the back. She turns to look at her supposed victory. Too late! As she looks down she realizes that Dante is holding his sword aimed at her, low on his haunches and ready to strike with lightning speed.

"It's a locked situation it seems." she says.

Dante winks and sweeps his leg around, knocking out the feet beneath Ragel. The tactical knife drops to the floor next to Ragel, breathing hard after the dropping on her back and hitting her head.

"Always keep your anger in check," Dante states calmly." We are not in this to show off, we're here to survive."

Dante moves towards his clothing hung up at his closet. Ragel slowly regains her composure and gets back to her feet.

"The girl you brought in." Ragel states

Dante continues without much attention to the conversation.

"Is she a rebel?" she asks.

Dante nods with his head. He turns to Ragel now standing close to him.

"Don't look at me like that." Dante says." She is a hostage just like any other. She will go through interrogation like all the others. If we're lucky we might get some worthwhile information from her" he says.

Ragel reaches down to Dante's hand before looking into his eyes.

"Don't get too close".

"It's my job to find their camp." Dante says.

He pulls away his hand and makes his way through the gym room, his sword on his side.

Dante walked out of the room, headed west towards the prisoner cells and purposely walked past Ophelia's room, telling himself it was just to check on the status of her latest report in the files. But he lingered longer than usual at her gate, watching her sleep. The room was dark and musty with a single metal framed bed and sheet-thin mattress. A bucket sat in the corner, ready for the prisoner to relieve herself. The room was infested with rat droppings, amongst other waste. He looked away and the next moment two guards, Privates Kyle and Shawn, walked by dragging between them a fighting hostage. The guy was dressed plainly in track pants that was stained and torn and a shirt that showed off a man built like a Rugby Player. He had an air around him as he looked straight at Dante before spitting on Dante's boots. Dante walked away as the one guard smashed his baton into the prisoner's ribs. It was less of a prison and more a POW camp. You were a source of information, a slave worker at most. If you made trouble, you were taken back behind the chemical shed and shot by six guards.

Philip glared at the man dressed in black. This soldier had an authority around him that the two men carrying him didn't. He despised men like that. Back in his wretched cell, he did various strange stretches to keep his muscle memory intact and his mind from becoming unhinged. He knew it was only a matter of time before they came for him. He just had to be strong, and wait it out. The sound of the metal gate opening made it clear. They were here and wanted something. He has outweighed his value, he had to speak or it will very well be his last day. Philip was able to distract the interrogators, tossing useless information at them, true to some extent, but not much more than a wild goose chase after his clan.

They took him into a large empty room with a single chair in the middle. The room was warm and suffocating. The midday sun was beating down into the room and dust filled the air. By the dark marks on the floor it was clear that others just as strong as him have died here. Their dried blood the only remnant left to tell their story, their bravery. Philip was tied to the chair and the men left the room. He sat there sweat dripping from his forehead in the blistering room. He would wait it out, he had broken many a bone before, what was a few more to keep safe the friends who were like family to him. It felt like hours before the door finally opened, one of the guards entered, walking straight towards him. The man looked him up and down before punching him in the stomach. Philip held back a grunt of pain.

"I like to start with pain first, so you know I am not bluffing." said Casper.

Philip glared at him, slowly working at the knots tying his hands together.

"I haven't had breakfast yet." whispered Philip.

Casper swung a fist connecting with his jaw. Philip laughed and spat out blood.

"That the best you got, pansy?" Philip mocked him.

"Where are they? Tell me their plans, whereabouts and no more sidetracking…"

Silence from Philip. Casper has gone through many prisoners before, and has always been able to break them, one way or the other. At the very least, they died in his attempt at extracting information.

———

After a half hour of beating and no response, Casper called in a young woman with a glass of water. She walked over nervously. It was clear that she was new. She was provocatively dressed in a tight black corset top, hardly breathing, walking around for morale of the military men, especially Casper. He liked his girls to be dressed up to his taste. Luxury clothing most women on the outside could not find easily. Casper took a sip and spat it out, throwing the glass to the ground.

"That tastes disgusting! Get out of my sight!" shouted Casper. She moved to the side, knowing his rage. Philip looked at her with a mix of contempt and pity. She wasn't like the women on the outside. She was meek and sheepish. A toy for boys with guns... She was most probably taken by force from her family at a young age. The door opened again and an unrecognizable military man walked in. Casper didn't recognize him. Turning around, Casper saluted the Sergeant-as indicated by the military badges on his uniform. Standing within close range from each other, Philip could see past Casper, recognizing the man standing there. The room went quiet. Casper was unsure of what the man wanted. No words escaped his mouth. The next moment the man, better known as Sam, leader of the Sabotage clan, hit Casper's feet out from beneath him with a standard billy club. Casper fell to the floor, banging his head against hard concrete floor. Philip by this time had already been able to get his hands free, waiting for the opportune moment. Now was as good as any he knew, and time was no luxury as the news will be out soon. They had to get out of here, fast. Philip jumps over Casper and hastily makes his way out of the room with Sam. His ribs hurt with every step but freedom was around the corner. They ran through the building, meeting up with one of the younger members, Clarence. Sam ran up the stairs and got the suspicion of a guard at the top, Philip by this stage was climbing up the rails next to the guard. As the guard moves his gun towards Philip, Sam throws a knife into the throat of the guard, attempting to silence the deathly blow to no avail as the limp body hits the ground with a thud. Another guard hears the noise in the next room and confronts Clarence, taking him down. Philip enters and takes down the guard with his body weight as he swings himself across the floor. It's too late for Clarence. It was clear as the tactical blade oozes with blood from his body. Their secret would be safe they knew, and they did not have time to take his body with them. There wasn't time for mourning, they had to keep moving.

Sam throws a strange sign with his arms, signaling for them to move out. The voice of Casper coming with other guards could be heard, as the sirens start going off. They have seconds before this side of the premises will be flooded with military. They sprint through the top level of the building, but the floor abruptly ends in open space. It is a two stories jump to the bottom level and they have no other escape route. Philip takes the chance and jump down, followed closely by Sam. Casper who was a few meters behind them at this stage stops at the floor's edge to look down on his prey as the men run away, out of the building. His furious shouting can be heard as the other soldiers start to arrive. But they're too late to shoot the two. And Casper gave chase without any weapons, as he didn't take any into the interrogation space.

Dante was sitting in his room cleaning his blade when he heard reports of the escaped prisoner. Not many have been able to leave the premises alive. Must have been someone with exceptional skills Dante thought, knowing their path will cross at some stage.

He walked out of his room and towards the cells. Ophelia was being dragged out of her cell wearing a white tight corset outfit. She did not shout, nor make a sound, even though it was clearly unpleasant. She was being taken to a room on the outskirts of the building, the one used for experimenting on prisoners. Dante followed close behind and into the room.

———

The room was white with a blood stained medical bed in the middle. There was a cabinet with a few odds and ends on it. In the other corner were cages full of rats. It was clearly not one of their top medical rooms, but it worked for the purpose of this exercise. Ophelia was silent as they strapped her to the bed and stuck a drip in her arm. He could see anger in her eyes, but otherwise she showed no other emotion. The doctor smiled and rearranged his tools as the interrogator James walked in. His smile was filled with pure sadistic intent as he looked at Ophelia like she was nothing more than a piece of fresh meat. He turned to look at Dante with disdain. He picked up a syringe filled with a strange concoction and approached Ophelia. Sliding the point of the needle slowly up her body as he spoke...

"You see this, my dear. This unique concoction is our latest creation which today we have the privilege of spreading through your entire body, stimulating your sympathetic nervous system until every single cell in your body experiences excruciating pain" he said in a cruel whisper.

He moves the medical instrument over her body, over the side of the kidney close to her breasts, seemingly taking pleasure in playing with his prey. James moves his face close to that of Ophelia's whispering into her ear.

"Unless of course, if you cooperate by telling us where your so-called 'fellow freedom fighters' are."

Ophelia turns away. Dante stands still and watches. Waiting to see where this will go.

"Then we proceed." James wheezes.

The scientist injects the syringe into her drip, squeezing the entire dosage into her.

"The thing is, your irregular warfare tactics are an irritation to the system. Hit and Run tactics, Sabotage, raids... futile." stated James.

Dante observes the procedures. He has seen many men and woman crack with James' procedures. The information was the key for him to track down their whereabouts. Dante did not particularly agree with the methods, but the outcome gave him a starting point and therefore he remained uninvolved throughout.

Ophelia doesn't respond. She bites back the pain. James leans down right by her face, his smirk evil.

"Tell me, thirsty?" question James.

The scientist pours water into her mouth. She looks straight at James and spit it into his face."

Increase the dosage" James says, slightly annoyed by his subject.

The scientist increase the dosage and she begins to fight it, her body shaking with pain, the sound of her breathing intensifying, her lungs moving as she gasps for air, before her convulsions turn so violent she goes into shock and passes out. The scientist feels her pulse.

"She is alive but it will take some time for her to regain consciousness." says the Scientist." You know I find it interesting that she remains alive whilst all the other Rebels were gunned down." states James.

James and Dante stand opposite each other next to Ophelia's body. The space is tense.

"You know I have been getting reports that organs have been

disappearing from cold storage. You wouldn't happen to know any-thing about that, would you?" ask Dante, his voice marked with suspicion.

They all look down at Ophelia.

"What a waste to kill all the Rebels while we need bodies for organs." sigh the Scientist.

"You can have her, when I am done with her." smile James.

"It is such a waste to use such a pretty face for experimentation." says the Scientist.

"Trust me, this face won't be as pretty when I am done with it." answer James.

They both laugh. James is at pleasure with his power in this space, and Dante merely a soldier reporting for duty under his command here.

"Take her, Commander. We can continue with this charade tomorrow morning. But I want to whip out some of the older methods. I find when it comes to woman, skinning works best."

James and the Scientist leave the room. Dante unstraps Ophelia, her arms bruised by the leather straps that held her down. The straps were linked into her corset top. Dante looks at her motion-less body and gently lifts her limp body into his arms. He walks out of the room.

4

Born of
Gods and Monsters"

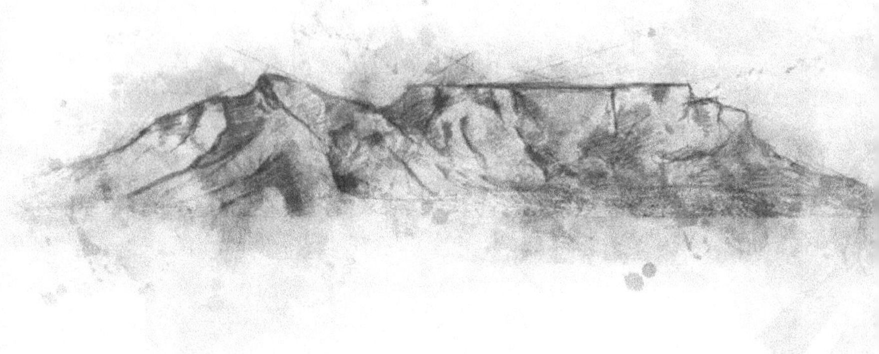

Dante walked into Ophelia's cell. She felt small in his arms fragile and innocent it seemed, yet so strong. Dante shook the thoughts away. He was tough and no woman would complicate his life, not even Ragel was able to get through he thought to himself. He laid her onto the metal framed bed with the pathetic mattress as she slowly awoke. Her eyes searched his, but found nothing safe for stoic resolve.

"Why do you keep fighting?" ask Dante.

"Why do you?" was her retort.

The room is quiet as Dante stands next to her thinking about her question directed at him." Is there really something still out there worth fighting for?" question Dante sitting down She slowly sat up, showing no signs of the pain that would be radiating through her body. Her white skin however shows the medication took the body into a state of shock. Her skin covered in red blotches.

"When you look into the eyes of a child, what do you see?" ask Ophelia.

Dante was not used to being asked these kinds of questions. Commands, allegations, threats, these were more likely to come to him.

"Sadness ..." His immediate response

He was staring out at the wall ahead, lost into a world unknown. Ophelia puts her hand over his, he looks down. His hand warm against her cold hand.

"I see a future, not livestock." She breathes deeply and tries to find his eyes.

His eyes are distant like a man who'd seen many horror stories.

"Deep inside, before you go to sleep, you tell them a story. You talk of a place with green fields, with water, a place where people can be so much more than barbaric and savage, for a few mere drops." whisper Ophelia.

She stares at the hard lines of his face. She had seen these types of faces many times before. Coming to the camps carrying hatred, carrying others' thoughts... He looked at her with confusion, which was probably new to him. She could see in Dante he was not completely lost. She remembers the faces of Emile, the people at her outpost, the baby…

"You need to help me, help me get back to my people." reply Ophelia.

Dante realizes that her emotional response is a trap, a setup to use him and he shuts down." This isn't a negotiation. You will remain here until further use for you is determined." Dante's stoicism softens, he looks at Ophelia. Reading her face, her eyes... She looks tired. The sun had opened her pores ever so slightly, toning her skinny frame. Dante remains still, his hand softly landing on Ophelia's wrist. His grip tightens. Dante rips Ophelia's hand from his wrist, holding his comm-watch. He calmly puts his other hand over hers, and snatches back his watch in irritation. Before Ophelia could reply, Ragel entered the room.

"Bennett is looking for you, we've spotted The Rebels." says Ragel.

She looked between the two of them. Dante stood up and

walked out without so much as a backward glance. Ragel stands at the door looking at Ophelia. She could sense something was up and did not like it at all. She however did not report the matter, kept it off file.

———————

Dante sat on the stairs leading to the bed he rarely used. His room was clean, packed with the aesthetic detail of a Soldier. The world was full of dirt but everything inside smelt like pine gel. Clean with white walls and everything straight and in its place. He had a military cabinet filled with personal effects: his boots, base uniform, his rifle and ammunition for his pistol along with a whetstone and rag to keep his sword sharp.

Bennett walked into the room, the hair at the temples of his head white. Dante stood up fastening his tactical vest, he walked up to Bennett who began to clip the back closed for him. Dante's mentor from his academy days, stood there looking at Dante with an air of concern.

"What's on your mind, son?" he asked.

"No it's nothing, don't worry about it." Dante walked towards the door, Bennett touched his shoulder.

"It'll get easier." said Bennett.

No further words were uttered. Bennett watched Dante walk away, and sat on the steps lighting his pipe. The man's best days were behind him. Soon he'll be discharged and a replacement be promoted to his old post. For a moment, he ponders his future ahead, wondering how Dante would do as Commanding Officer.

A group of men, seemingly Rebels, were busy loading up water down at an abandoned reservoir. How they retrieved it was unknown. Dante knew they had to confiscate it, and get information. Any source of water, how little it might be, stood in the way of their control of the territories. It would lead to political hell and their claim towards the building of a better society scattered by fortune hunters growing powerful with this hidden source. Dante watched from a distance, his eyes trained on the men. He moves in taking down one of the men standing on guard, quietly cutting his throat. The military move in proper tactical lay out, shooting out the guards within a few moments. The rest of the people trying to escape or fight back, are gunned down within seconds. Rifles at the ready, they sweep the area. It was dark and the cold was seeping through his uniform. The military move into formation to guard the area whilst Dante goes through the information. He calls in to the main station, letting them know the area has been secured. It was unceremoniously quiet. The military guard stood watch inside the crumbling building, from out of the vents behind him slipped another Rebel. She quietly grabs him from behind, slitting his throat. The next moment a group of them come out from different hiding places and ambush the military. The military fires blindly, killing them off, their numbers large but weapons quite futile and archaic. A few military men drop down as someone from the top shoots at them with an AK47. The blasts echo around them as gun fire goes off. Rebels fall to the ground. The next moment a large flame erupts and a bomb explodes where Dante has been standing. Dante drops to the floor and sees more rebels moving in. The loud sound disorientates him, throwing all his senses out of whack. He sees a stream of blood next to his body and struggles to push himself up with his arm. Two of the Senior Officers pick him up, if he is captured, all will be lost. The rest of the military stand their ground as the Rebels surround them, like ants moving in on a slowly dying spider. Dante struggles to get to his gun to shoot but he is powerless, his body moves into a state of shock and darkness envelops around him.

———————

Ophelia stands on weak legs as she walks towards the wall. She picks up a piece of glass and stares at it. She imagines the blood run down as she contemplates ending it this way before they do it for her. She sighs and hears the sound of other prisoners crying, some shouting in pain. What has the world come to? She kneels down in her dress, covered in filth. Feeling elegant for once in her life… She knew that even this dress was a way of torturing them, giving them a sense of peace, of beauty before tearing it away. These psychological games were often used as bait, to lure them in, to give up, to give over. The worst place to ever feel elegant in she knew. But this outfit was better than any she had worn before. She looked at the wall before her, a tear running down her cheek as she starts to hum a tune she remembers her mother singing to her as a child. She remembers every single face before her, especially the ones that had died too young. The ones that had been lost to a war they should have never been fighting. She wishes she could recall her mother, or her father. But she can't even recall their names.

<hr>

Dante opened his eyes, pain radiating from a limb that was clearly missing. He looked around his room. Ragel sat staring at him in the corner. Concern in her eyes as she stared down at him... Dante tried to pick up his body, hearing a different sound, feeling a different weight to his arm. A black mechanical arm has replaced his left arm. Still strapped into bandages Dante's at a loss for words. Ragel fought back tears. He looked back at her with hard eyes, barely showing any emotion at the loss of his arm. She wanted to comfort him, show him she cared. She moved closer to him, to touch him. She herself was in shock, believing he wasn't going to make it out alive. She has been next to him throughout the whole process. Dante withdrew from her touch.

"How long have I been out?" Dante croaked
His voice hoarse, from screaming he didn't remember. She

however recalled his shouting as he came in that night, his arm in shreds, blood pouring on the floor. If it had not been for their large blood bank he would not have made it through the night. She heard him shouting names she hasn't heard before, his eyes were distant and he didn't see her. It was as if he has already left this space. She was crying softly when he woke up. Quickly wiping away the tears before he noticed… He would not want her to be soft, not even for him. To let down your guard is weak. Ragel rush closer to him, wanting to lay a hand on his arm, realizing it was metal, she hesitates. He struggles upright to regain some composure in front of Ragel and mistakenly leans on his ghost arm. The metal arm is nothing like his real one. Nothing like flesh and bone... He resents the fact that he looks weak in front of her. Dante fights the fever raging through him and sits up. He lifts the metal arm and attempts to bend it. Ragel opens her mouth to say something, but stop at the last second. He slowly lifts it and move one finger. Dante tries to hide the pain and shame. Why did they not let him die? Now he felt like half a man. Dante looks down at his bandaged and raw flesh and sighs. This was going to be his new life. He finally moves the hand and sees the warm smile Ragel gives him. He feels nothing but pain and cold. His mind tells him there is an arm still there, but he can see there is none. A radiating pain shoots through him and he groans.

"You just need to rest." said Ragel.

"How many did we lose?" Dante asks through gritted teeth.

Ragel looks away, tears in her eyes.

"It was a confusing situation, none of the men saw it coming, you couldn't…"

"How many?" interupts Dante angrily

"Most of them…"

Dante wipes the sweat from his forehead.

"I need to get medication." replies Dante, barely reacting to the notion of all his men and brothers lost to the Rebels.

"It's fine, Just rest. I'll get it for you." answers Ragel moving away from him.

Dante wants her to do it, but he has had enough of weakness. He does what he needs to save face.

"Leave me alone." growls Dante storming out the room. The metal arm hangs limp against his side. Dante never meant to hurt her, and feels sorry for a moment. She was his friend, or closest thing he ever had to that in here. They've spent a lot of time together, grew up together. He's been her strength and she has been good to him. Dante struggles to focus as he walks, trying to find his way to the lab.

Ophelia looks around the room, her body strapped to the uncomfortable and cold bed. The room is chilly and she feels goosebumps rising. The doctor is preparing instruments as James smiles with twisted glee. Ophelia spots the small Protea in a glass case, recognition sparkling in her eyes. The doctor notices what she is looking at and locks it away in the metal cabinet. He places the key on the tray with the tools. James starts drawing dots with a pen on her face where he plans on cutting. It looks like a marked out operation, along the face lines. He picks up the blade and pushes down. Blood trickles out as Dante walks into the room.

"Aren't you supposed to be in the ICU, soldier?" ask James looking up at Dante.

James stops for a moment, taking pleasure in knowing he is in control here. The story of Dante's loss has gone through the camp. Most respectably show their tribute to the loss of other men. James however uses it as a point to better himself, to stand tall above Dante, the legend as they call him. The doctor and James laugh. Dante stares at them for a moment smiling along sarcastically and quickly changes his face to a serious state between pain and anger.

"You seem to enjoy playing with your toys." Dante looks James straight in the eye.

His head throbs with pain. All he wants is some medication and to leave this space.

"Remember you are the one responsible for bringing us the prey" James says finding pleasure in the fact.

Ophelia's eyes track them.

"I risk my life out there. While you hide here like rats." retorts Dante.

By the sound of it, James seems to be delighted.

"So you're the hero? Then tell me Commander, most of your men are dead and you are still here. Why? Did you hide away?" ask James stepping into Dante's space."Like a coward." spat James.

Dante chuckles for a moment. He kicks the scientist in the gut, flooring the weak man. He grabs James by the throat with his robotic hand and squeezes. The hand was fast, strong. James had little of a chance. Trying to pry open the metal fingers around his throat, James passes out as Dante turns to face Ophelia. James' blade drops to the floor with a reverberating clang. Dante doesn't know why he is doing this. But he has to help her. He quickly loosened the straps and helps to lift her off the bed. She is weak, but has the determination to live.

"You okay? We have to get out of here." states Dante helping her to her feet.

Nothing made sense to him anymore, and he has just placed himself in a very dangerous place attacking another officer in the military. She looks towards the cupboard and attempts to break free from his hold.

"Wait, no, wait. I can't leave without it. It's the Adam's seed!"

Dante ignore her and tries to move her out of the room before the others regain consciousness.

"I am not leaving!" cry Ophelia.

Dante walks with her towards the cupboard and searches for the key. But in the struggle it must have been knocked to the ground. He grabs the door with his robotic arm and rips it open. Ophelia gently takes the glass container and turns to leave with Dante.

"Come we have to go." He orders

They make their way out of the room that held so much death in it. He was sure that what was ahead would bring doom, staying would just hasten it.

5

And the Rivers shall
run red with blood

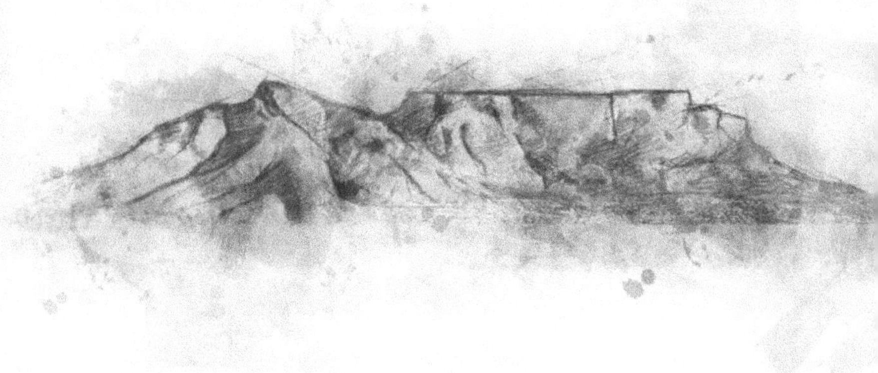

Dante and Ophelia walked as quiet as possible past the last few guards and made their way out of the compound. They were walking in the silent of the night, carrying the Protea. They found their way out to the outside of the building.

"Be quiet, stay low and don't fall behind." whispered Dante.

Ophelia looked down at the Protea and then grabbed Dante's arm. Stopping them from walking any further…

"Promise me if something happens to me, you will give this to my people." pleaded Ophelia.

"Keep it quiet." Ordered Dante

"Promise me, promise me." She pleaded again

Dante looked down at her hand on his arm and relented with a quiet nod. He took the Protea and put it in his pocket.

"I promise. Now please, we have to get out of here. Keep moving." replied Dante

He took her arm and gently pulled her forward. She bit back the pain as glass and stones cut into her bare feet. The air was freezing and she wore the ugly corset. She felt exposed, she felt wounded and she felt lost. But most importantly she felt determined, with a renewed sense of purpose. Dante had come for her and he had lost his arm, she saw the pain in his face. He tried to hide it but he couldn't as the fresh wound started to bleed through the meatal and gauze. Dante had lost a piece of himself, he felt incomplete, hollow. He hoped helping Ophelia escape would redeem his past transgressions. Perhaps that would fill the void he now felt. He knew he would be able to speak to Bennett. Find his way back in, even if it meant severe punishment. But right now, he couldn't think about going back. All he held dear was changed, ripped apart at the core. His belief of what he was fighting for stood as a question, no longer a clear thought or dream. The world was not better, not in here nor out there. Dante was hoping he could find what Ophelia had, that sense of hope she followed blindly.

They reach a large concrete platform. The exit was so close, within throwing distance. The sound of the alarm echo through their heads, they could hear the jack-booted guards in a running march. Ophelia grabs onto Dante, he's looking for a way out. He tries to lift his arm but it's not working. Then he sees Ragel pointing a gun at him, silently pleading for him to come quietly. Once allies, Dante looks around him as his former brothers-in-arms encircle the two. The irony suddenly becomes clear to both sides. He would bargain with them, but their rifles are pointed at him. Ophelia clambers behind him like a frightened child. Dante knows they won't shoot him, their Commander. He will be arrested and taken to face up to what he has done at a court martial. This was enough to give her a chance. He takes a step forward and suddenly, without warning a gunshot is heard. He reacts, but not fast enough as he sees Ophelia dive in front of him. Everything slows to a crawl. Dante looks down at her writhing body. He kneels down and picks up her fragile figure. She looks up at him, blood seeping onto her corset and marble skin. She clutches the wound looking at him. He drops to his knees, feeling for the first time in his life real raw pain. He knows the wound is fatal, knows that she won't make it. She moves her hand slowly towards his neck trying to pull him down. Sadness replaces anger. The only family he knew had killed the only good thing, the only honest thing, he had ever found. She had given him a strange sense of hope. He never asked for it, yet she gave it freely. Someone who made him feel after death almost stole his heart.

"Please." whispers Ophelia, the last breath leaving her as a single tear ran down her cheek. The look of murder in Dante's eyes the last thing she would ever see. Standing up slowly, he leaves her body on the floor. If ever there was hope for him, it was gone now with her last breath. He took one last look at Ragel, and then quickly stepped forward. The soldiers' eyes widened and before they could fire again, he had grabbed one of the young new recruits and had his arm around the neck and gun pointed at him.

"Please Dante." cried Ragel.

Dante dragged the whimpering soldier into the darkness with him, already planning his escape. He knocked the soldier out, wanting to kill him for killing Ophelia. He should just do it; this boy had taken something worth more than anything anyone could even comprehend. He was about to kill him when he heard footsteps. So he finished him quickly and moved on.

Even while ill and not able to walk properly, he still made it unseen into his room. Dante collected his sword and gun and with one last look walked out.

"Stop or we shoot." screamed an officer.

"Shoot, you heartless bastards!" yelled Dante.

An unexpected officer rounded the corner and Dante grabbed him, holding the sword to his side. Bennett stepped out of the shadows of the long corridor.

"Dante, let's talk about this." said Bennett.

"There's no point in talking now, no good comes from your version of peaceful negotiation." replied Dante.

Bennett signaled for everyone to leave them alone. He looked at Dante, the boy he had practically raised.

"Why are you doing this?" asked Bennett taking a step closer.

"Because people like you are the reason that people like them exist in the first place." Dante pressed the sword into his hostage's side. The soldier let out a cry of pain.

"You said it yourself, we're Cattle Wranglers. They're cattle." Said Bennett.

"I am going to walk out of here and you're gonna let me…" said Dante backing towards the door. Bennett took out his gun and aimed it at Dante's head.

"Don't do this Dante, where will you go? What will you do if you continue on this path?"

"Better out there than in here. At least I won't have to be a trained mutt." said Dante while stepping back

Bennett looked him in the eyes.

"You're one of us." Said Bennett lowering his gun

"She didn't matter. The Officers you took down though, we can't take this offense lightly." Snarled Bennett.

"I was one of you. Not anymore. Not ever again." stated Dante stabbing the soldier from the back right through his heart, dropping his body to the floor.

Bennett aimed his gun at Dante, but didn't shoot as Dante made his way out of the compound.

The one place he had called home for so many years. He walked out and didn't look back. A life for a life he thought. The price of freedom was only his soul. They followed Dante and he had to fight for his life now, being tracked over the hills into the desert space. He knew this was his only chance. His body was butchered by fever, cuts from various blades and a gunshot wound to the shoulder. The wind was blowing strongly and Dante headed into the sand storm, creating distance between him and those who followed. Into uncharted territory, where most who dared go in, never came out again. Bennett stayed back watching Dante disappear into the storm. He called back his men who were firing shots into the storm.

The light was dimming fast. Dante crawled most of the way, his open wounds bleeding profusely, deluded from his rising fever and blood loss. He braced himself with his arms but the robotic one was still not working efficiently. He had a thirst beyond anything he ever knew, probably from the pain of clinging to life. His lungs were burning. He stood up, seeing demons of the past, a boy who could not save himself. A man who was worse than death, Dante refused to back down. He swung his sword forward, physically fighting the invisible demon. He used most of his energy fighting the entity. A man he refused to name, a man he hated with all his heart. He fell to his knees, out of breath and on the brink of death. His wounds were infected, sand in parts of the rawness where gauze had failed to cover. He looked to the sky. The sun had come up and with it a harshness that had caused dehydration to take its toll.

"Curse you." Muttered Dante falling face first into the sand The protea in one hand and the sword still covered in dry blood and sand in the other.

The last thing Dante recalls seeing was that of a strange sight. A yellowish-brown skinned man walking over the dunes, holding what seemed to be a bow and arrow. Dante felt he was being picked up, but had no strength to fight back.

Dante was near death. He might not survive, but they were going to try. They had seen too many die out there and if one life could be saved then their work was done. They carried the body, it took three of them. The leader had said they must bring back something of value, was a man's life valuable? They walked, sticks in hand, sandals of leather made from the hides of animals, hunted for food and clothing. This man was of no color to them, even though he was mzungu. They carried him through the desert, to a hidden village far from anything and anyone. Villagers stood staring as they carried the wounded man towards the chief. The chief looked down at the man and nodded his head. They carried him towards the sick hut and laid him down.

Over the next few days there were quite a few close calls. They had to do some intense burning of flesh around the metal arm to clear infection. They worked hard to save Dante. He was a man marked for death. But death to these people was merely a passage and they are often in a state of dance around the fire for anyone who would move over beyond this world of living. He woke a few times in a state of delirium, screaming in pain. On one occasion, he even awoke and grabbed a young woman by the neck, but was swiftly knocked down by a guard. It was a dark time for Dante. He finally awoke almost a week later, having lost quite a bit of weight, but the infection was gone. The skin around his robotic arm was slowly scarring. He accepted a sip of fresh cactus rose water from a young woman and looked around the room. The taste was something new to Dante. It was warm yet sweet. Dante was in a large hut. The ground was hard and the light in the room came from candles made from God knows what. Dante was confused from what had happened during the last week. He looked sideways and saw his sword and the protea lying there. Dante grabbed his sword and slowly stood up. His legs were weak from not being used. An elderly man followed by a younger man walked into the hut, they both stared straight at Dante making their way towards him. Dante didn't know what to say to these people, but he knew that they had saved his life. He took a wobbly step towards them. The elderly man could only be the chief by the way he held himself, and the way everyone in the hut looked at him. The chief stepped forward, the younger man by his side. He started speaking in his native tongue. Dante stood still trying to figure out what the chief was saying. He finally stopped talking and Dante held out his hand for a handshake.

"Thank you for helping me…" said Dante

The chief looked down at Dante's hand and walked away.

6

A Day no
Pigs Would Die

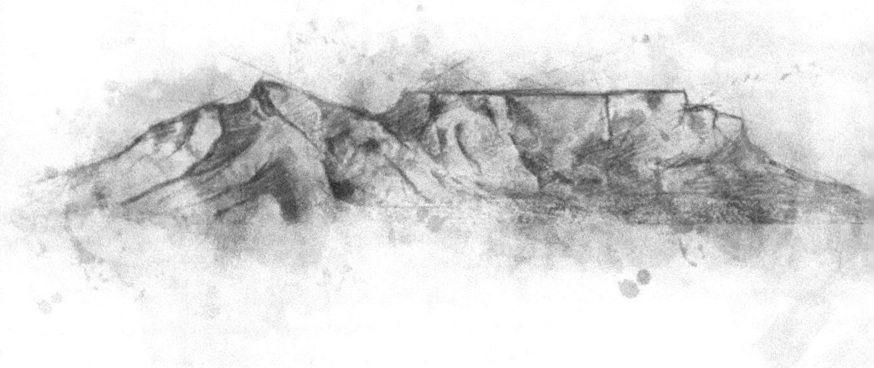

Dante worked closely with the younger tribe members. They were kind to him for some reason. Dante did not understand their way of living, let alone their language. He quickly came to learn that his world was not theirs. What was of value to him had no value to them. The little he had on him they kept aside, even away from the curious children. They had no use for possessions or anything that would give a man the idea of superiority. They were nomadic and pure. Their way of life remained untouched by the strife of industry. Their language proved problematic to understand, but communication was achieved by body language and mimicry. They showed him many survival tricks and helped him gain his strength back. Dante knew he was being watched closely by the elders but he was grateful for what they had done and was more than willing to learn. He was out on his own now and the world was not a friendly place. He had lived very sheltered in the way that there was always food and water. Here they dug up roots for food and used archaic tools to bring water out of the ground. Dante wanted to be able to talk to them, thank them properly. Instead he became the student and let the masters teach him. He realized they do not have a leader, and that they rule as a group. They did not want power or respect, as he was used to.

He silently watched these people, their community and the strength of their relationships, rarely heard of in the real world. The San people of the old times, hunted down in the 1800's with very few surviving. Those who did not keep to their old way of life had to become part of the modern societies. Yet here he was with a group that somehow kept to traditionalism, and they had survived without violence. They had weapons used for hunting only. They thanked the gods for every meal and made offerings in return. They were shadows of men, the women working to help gather supplies and the men hunting, whilst children played, oblivious to the cruelty of the world. Dante had been here a few weeks now and was facing his last task, they had all gone hunting and had left him, the temperature was dropping and his stomach was complaining. He would survive tonight and show them they had taught him well. He found a cave to hide in and wait the night out.

Philip looked over at Sam and Jenny, his bruises had healed nicely and the souvenirs from the last raid had made them a lot richer. Jenny was the voice, where Sam was a mute, Jenny would interpret. Sam had raised her, and was like a brother. No one knew why he didn't talk, no one asked questions. Jenny was tall and athletic, with toned muscles from working out. She wore the typical leather bands from Sabotage. She was a strong warrior. Philip had thought himself in love with her, but that was just admiration for her loyalty to Sam. Sam took them from the dirt. They were torn to pieces, thrown in the gutter and left to die.

But he taught them to fight and to survive. He taught them to make fear their friend and face every new height as an adventure as you leapt across a roof. It was night and they were covered head to toe, Philip was armed with a pair of garden shears taken apart and sharpened into crude knives. He had them in his belt, at his back. Following behind were three boys, no older than twelve. They were dirty and alone, and followed Sam around like ducklings. Philip would help train them. Jenny would help nurture them. And in a few years, they would grow into young men hardened by the unforgiving landscape. They were saved from becoming playthings to a cruel, beastly group of men. Sam was their hero. Sam was everyone's hero, the silent and deadly protector. A lone wolf with his litter of cubs... The boys were cold and scared. But Jenny was a source of warmth in every sense. She would smile and pull funny faces at the boys. The youngest would giggle at her so loudly, that you could see his missing teeth. Philip could see they were getting tired, but it was not safe out here. They saw a cave, but it was too open, anyone could spot them from a fair distance. Philip heard a sound in the still of the night. He flashed his torch towards the cave. Sam stopped and looked at him. Philip waited, with nothing but the shivers of the boys emanating in the air. He shrugged his shoulders and they carried on walking. They finally reached a set of abandoned buildings near morning. Someone flew across from a roof into a window in the opposite building. Philip smiled. It was good to be home. They were at their training camp, roughly twelve days' walk from their home base in the former city of Cape Town. Once a glorious urban sprawl, named for design capital, the city of the future, now a picturesque vision of hell. Cape Town was a constant reminder of man's failures, crawling with all manner of dangerous individuals.

A few heads peeked out suspiciously from a window and saw them approaching. They jumped from the first story window down onto the ground. Sam's face lit up at the sight of the young boys running towards them. The older ones walked at a slower pace, not wanting to appear too excited. Sam dropped down the three large dead animals and held his arms open for the young boys. It was clear from the figure of these animals they had been exposed to the effects of radiation. But this was as good a meal as any. Resources were beyond scarce and most people's bodies have found a way to adapt to the poisons the earth was soaking in. A man steps forward and inspects the food closely by cutting open the stomach to look at the color. He smells it and smiles. It seems a perfect meal to celebrate.

Two of the children, the youngest, were only five and had been there for a year now. They were twin boys who had been found in a sewer pipe starving and huddled together like cowering pups. Sam was the father they never had. Philip became their brother who trained them. No one got a free ride, they worked hard for supplies. Traders by nature, taking and giving in equal shares. But they knew that to survive, sometimes bad things had to happen. They had to kill when necessary, but Jenny was always there to nurture them from the fallout. Philip took the one twin Jacob and lifted him onto his shoulders.

"Howzit bud? Meet the newest recruits. Lyle, David and Ezra." said Philip pointing to the boys staring at everyone warily.

"Can we show them." whispered Jacob in Philip's ear.

"Hmm, I am not sure they're ready." replied Philip.

The youngest, Lyle stepped forward.

"I am ready." answered Lyle.

"Alright, follow the boys and don't be scared, you're safe here." Declared Philip putting Jacob down

His twin brother Caleb gave him a high five and ran off, calling the boys to follow. The twelve year old Ezra stayed behind.

"Don't you want to go with them?" asked Jenny. Ezra shook his head, hair hanging over his eyes, dirty and oily. They walked through the abandoned building, falling apart and hidden from others. Philip pointed out a few living quarters till they arrived at the main building. Sam and Jenny walked away leaving Philip with the latest recruit. He looked at Ezra, the boy was almost as tall as him.

"I saw what you can do." said Philip

"What?" Ezra questioned

"Come in, I'll show you."

Philip led Ezra to a building not far from where they were. He walked under an archway and into an exercise room. The room was filled with empty crates built at different levels. There were firemen poles and ledges with old worn mattresses below. There was makeshift equipment all over.

"Show me what you got." stated Philip.

The boy smiled for the first time and traversed the obstacles with relative ease. Philip had missed the training a lot, soon they were working up a sweat, jumping and flipping, flying and rolling. They heard clapping and looked up to see Jenny standing there.

"Well done boys, the food's getting cold." she said walking away.

Philip patted Ezra on the shoulder."Welcome home, brother."

A few days had passed and the boys were settling in well. Philip was ready for the next raid. He said his goodbyes to everyone then walked towards Sam. He shook his hand and walked away. Philip preferred walking at night, but the urge to explore was too strong. Using buildings as his guide, he leapt from rooftop to rooftop. He looked out for any dangers and kept a vigil eye on whatever he could gain from trading what he had with him, two bottles of clear water. Philip leapt across a building and rolled to his feet, he climbed down and walked through the streets. He loved his life, yes it was scary at times but the thrill was what enticed him. It was morning and people were crowding all over. Philip slipped past a few people, stealing a few items from them as he went. A coin here or there, jewelry and anything else he could take. Philip barely looked around, intent on what he was doing. He approached a tall man with a robotic arm and tried to take a pouch off of him. The man, Dante, turned and faced him. Philip recognized the face and fear ran through him. The man was looking at him, trying to place him. There was a loud commotion off to the side and Philip took the opportunity and scurried off.

Dante was sure he had seen the young man before, he just couldn't place him. A face from the past... Dante turned towards the commotion on his left, but the crowd was large enough to obstruct his view. He turned back and the young man was gone. The long travel through the desert took Dante through various towns, mostly abandoned. This one was populated though. It had road signs rusted over time. Next to the road, cars were covered in thick layers of dirt and grime, barely their shapes remained, parts broken off to be melted or repurposed. Bodies in various states of decay lay scattered over the roads. A sickly dog was busy chewing on some of the bones. With no place or clear direction where to go, Dante's only leads were but a few words and a vague sense of direction. He made his way through the streets, past the burnt and collapsed buildings. Some seemed nice enough for a night's shelter. Furniture and elements of old remained in some empty buildings. Anything of real use had already been taken. Dante could sense he was being watched as he walked down the street. Eyes were staring down at him from atop a building, like a vulture. The town was open for outsiders, to trade, but kept a tight watch on the scene. Dante saw the shining metal shimmer from a higher building, clearly a gun from a watchman.

Dante scouts around to see if there might be anything of use to him, but the place has basically been cleaned out. Once a small populated town, the name on the board can hardly be seen any-more, Victoria West. Some of the buildings could be clearly seen dating back from the early 1900's, maybe even earlier. They've seen better days than these. With little time and resources, people could hardly preserve their own lives, let alone the buildings. Some hardened people refused to leave the place they call home. It was a perfect place for a discreet meeting, to do a quick trade or find some information. That was exactly what he was looking for. Dante walked for days to get here. He walks through the wide streets. An old hotel bar situated at the end of the road seems to be popular. Dante walks through the doors and can sense all eyes staring down on him. Out here people don't trust strangers. Inside the cool air was refreshing compared to the scorching sun. Everyone stopped to look at the stranger for a second before going on with their daily activities. Various groups of people sat around the tables, gambling away any valuable items they have. An archaic system of trading took the form of currency. A bullet can buy you a shot of what seems like clear ethanol, and clear water will get you a whole bottle of presumably moonshine. Most alcoholic beverages were crudely homebrewed and had various uses from cleaning infected wounds to stripping rust off useful metal parts.

Dante walks towards the bar and place down six bullets, military grade and basically new. The bartender inspects the bullets closely and nods his head.

"What will it be?" ask the bartender.

Dante slides over a picture. The bartender looks at him and shakes his head. On the bar counter Dante draws the sigil of the rebel group the Commandos, the bartender flips the photo over face down on the counter and grabs a bottle of mampoer. It is always unclear on which side people are, until blood is shed. Those who support the Commandos know better than to share any information about them. Dante looks around. Two men sit together at the far end, one with a washed out torn blue jean and no shirt to hide his fat belly, and another sitting in an old grey shirt and faded pants, his dirty feet bare. They look ragged and cruel. Hardened killers... Easy targets for Dante... There are two more close to the door. Layered clothing makes it difficult to see what they are packing underneath. Dante almost never started a fight, but sure as hell always finished them. He first needed to find some info at least. Dante takes out shotgun shells from his bag. The atmosphere starts to grow tense, and a few people stare around as he does this. The man leans down and takes out a glass, not very clean. He pours water in it, to the top.

"Help yourself. But when you're done... find your way to another town." the barman uttered. Dante takes a gulp at the water. It was clear to Dante that he was not welcome here, even between the odd townspeople who claimed their place in this dying town. If it wasn't for the town being an in-between spot, it would have been completely deserted long ago already."He said there's nothing here for you." Bellowed a drunken lummox behind Dante

Dante turns around, looking up at the greasy heap with steely eyes. His hand slowly lowers towards his sword, tightening his grip. He decides to rather ignore him and starts walking towards the door. The man without a shirt steps in front of Dante, smirking. His stench so unbearable it could bring a tear to your eye. The man looks at Dante's bag.

"What else you got there? Brought me a present?" The shirtless man demands moving his hand towards the bag

In a swift movement, Dante unsheathes his sword and swings it in the man's direction, cutting off four of his fingers with surgical precision. The man stands there, his face going red as he screams in pain, blood gushing from the stumps.

"You backwater trash bags don't seem to understand!" Dante calls to attention all the patrons."I just came here for information, and now I'm leaving, with all of my things. If anybody even looks at me funny and I will cut off your genitals and feed it to the first mangy beast I see outside, while you watch." He said with booming authority.

The patrons grew so tense it was palpable.

"Now then, have a lovely day." Dante steps over the whimpering heap bleeding on the floor to exit the bar.

"When a man comes to our town, he normally brings us a

gift." another man says flashing a blade.

The man in grey responds,"It's just good manners. Drop down that bag and we might let you leave without bleeding too much".

Dante has heard many threats in his life. Big words were seldom backed up.

"Not in my bar!" yells the bartender.

The man with the blade moves towards Dante with intent to kill him. As quick as before, Dante relieves the man of his blade, and the arm attached to it. As the man drops to the floor, Dante's blade is back at his side. He looks at the other patrons with steely resolve, yet remains calm. The man's eyes rove around to see where his blade went. In the eyes of the knifeman Dante sees a shadow moving behind him. He quickly ducks down and the man swings past to hit his own friend with a broken bottle."The petrol sniffing sure didn't help with reflexes" Dante thought. Pandemonium erupts, men angry and ready to kill advance on him. Outside on the street people clear back into their shells of buildings, knowing it is better to stay out of trouble here. A violent brawl ensues. Blood spatters against the dusty windows as body parts and bladed weapons hit the floor in a wet squash.

As the violence dies down, the barman rises from behind his hiding spot. The crowd that attempted to sneak up and steal from Dante is all down, most not dead but injured to a degree not to fight with him at this point.

"I have no quarrel with you." the barman says to Dante.

Dante takes out a box from his bag and gives it to the man. The man looks inside and smiles."This should cover the damage and cleanup. You sure you don't know anything about them?" Dante asks again.

The man looks out to the far side of town.

"Have you ever heard of the Cape Mountains, van Hinks?" the man asks. Dante looks puzzled.

"There is a woman, Aurora. They say she can see the future, that she can see it all." The bartender says.

Dante looks the man straight in the eye.

"I don't need to see the future." Dante says.

"The world ended bad, the government swiped through here and left behind nothing but dust, the rest of the traders and tribes came through time after time, riots, fighting, most however did not die fighting the government. If you've seen it with your own eyes, you won't go looking for answers..." The barman's voice grew somber and dark as he was talking.

"I don't take interest in folklore." Dante says.

"These ain't no kid's stories." the barman warns"Most people tried to hide, their sounds, the cracking sound of fire as they move through, taking children and whatever they find useful. I have never seen so much blood."

The barman stands looking as if he sees it happening in front of his eyes.

"They leave behind a claw, after they come through."

This immediately interests Dante, as he has had many a run in with the Owl Clan while in the military.

"The rebels on the other hand have been good to us. I can tell you no more unfortunately, even if that means my life."

Dante looks at the barman for a moment, turns around and walks down the street. Didn't take long before Dante realized he was being followed. He walks around a building and stops after taking the corner. A young woman rounds the corner, black eye and swollen lip. She looks up at him confidently, but he can see the underlying fear there.

"What do you want?" asked Dante impatiently.

"My Husbands' head..."

7

The Great Devide

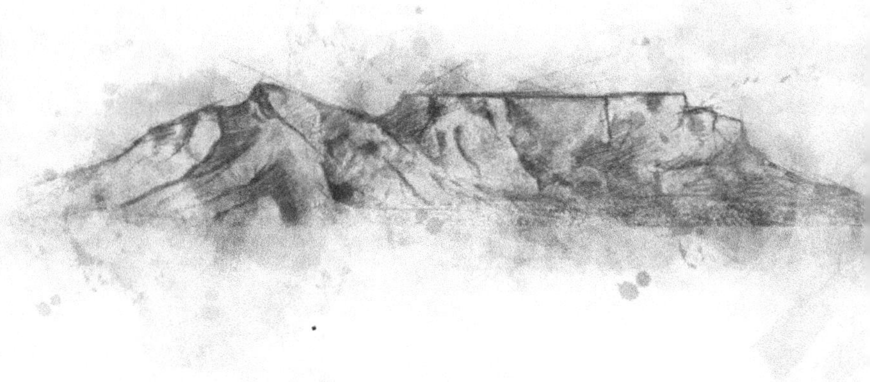

Dante stood looking down at the woman.

"Why would I do that?" asked Dante.

"Because I have information I'm willing to trade." said the woman.

Dante turned to walk away, but she grabbed his shirt again.

"Trust me. You'll want to hear what I have to say."

"I'm not a mercenary." answered Dante.

"He's a drunken womanizer. When he's had a little too much… It's like I'm his punching bag. Please do this." pleaded the woman.

"My heart bleeds for you Lady. Really, it does. But I don't see how…"

She turned around then slowly lifted her top, Dante noticed right away the same mark as Ophelia had seared into her bruised skin. The mark of the Rebels...

"You're a Rebel." Dante said with renewed intrigue.

"I was. Until I got kidnapped and forced to marry that Owl whisperer." said the woman.

"He sings the song of the owl. They take the children. They even took my own child. His only child... Please help me" She pleaded as she turned and walked away.

"I can't stand this town anymore." She said under heavy breath.

"I hate this place. Everyone calls me the Owl Girl. Catcalling and spitting. He's a beastly man. Just like his fellow clansmen".

She tried to run away before, twice. The last time they found her lying on the street, with shallow drill marks in the back of her head, a slow way to infuse pain. She was left in this state for a few days, mumbling, crawling without direction. She can't even remember the girl she was before. Many of these cruel acts Dante has seen before, commonplace in men with violent convictions. They had duty in their hearts, and stones in their hands. The sun seemed to vanish faster behind the hills bordering the town. With darkness come all kinds of terrors. That night the young girl was lying in bed, unable to fall asleep. Next to her was the Owl Clan member, already asleep in a drunken stupor. No honor in being the beast for sure.

———

Dante stood on the roof, biding his time. Ready to strike... The scars on her body a persistent thought. The lines of good and evil had been blurred to the point that he couldn't tell which was which. It was a clear target, a means to an end. He knew the game well. A simple exercise... Two men kept watch outside. An easy kill... He dispatches them with ease. Two rusty nails hit them square in the head, dropping them to the floor before they knew what had happened. Dante drops down from his perch as their limp bodies hit the ground. No noise. Small amounts of blood sputter from their skulls as he walks closer, raiding their bodies for anything worthwhile. He strips them of their extra ammo clips and medical field supplies."Easy Game" He thought. The big old building used to be a cinema it seems, projector equipment and old film negatives litter the once pristine tiled floors. Dante walks through the hall, the prestige rows of seats and cup holders covered in a fair amount of dust. The place had been left in disarray for years. On the blank white screen, the Owl Clan sigil was painted up high in red paint. At least, Dante hoped it was red paint. This was their hub, a makeshift gathering place for the scum of the earth. A sanctuary of the damned... From what Dante could tell, it hadn't been used in a while. Thin layers of dust danced over filthy cups and plates and the candles had taken on that greasy quality after a long period of not being in use. Something was up."Why would there be guards?" he thought. Dante walks towards the sound of someone snoring and makes his way up to the projector room. The man is laying in the projector room in deep slumber. Ready for a scuffle, he unsheathes his knife. It was a part of him, an extension of his hand, his sixth finger. It never faltered, never failed. Standing over the man, Dante smells his drunken breath, with her lying next to him. It is clear from his own appearance that he was marked by the Owl, scarring over his arms trailing up onto his neck, it showed his rank. He was high in the number, clearly had a name for killing. The man's eyes opened and instantly Dante hits the blade through the man's throat, silencing him. The girl wakes up frightened. Air and warm blood gushes from the wound. Dante's robot hand pushes the man down, keeping him in place. The kill was clean.

The girl shared what she knew about the Cape Commando, whatever Dante needed to know. He made mental notes of whatever useful information he could get out of her incoherent rambling. She knew it wouldn't be long before the sun would rise, and news spread like a plague in these cursed lands. She wasn't safe. She ran in hope of a better life, away from her jailers."Futile." Dante thought. He walked through this waste of a town, looking at the ruin of society."Where did it go wrong, who was to blame for this misery?" Dante mused to himself. He thought of life before this catastrophe. The beautiful intricacies... Everything he would never know. A sort of calmness in the humdrum of everyday existence... He didn't care that he killed the fat Owl man. He found a way to live for that matter, trading his skill as a killer for anything worthwhile, water; food; information, anything he needed. The one thing he knew how to do, better than anything else, was to kill. He looked at his robotic hand and sighed. It still felt like his real hand was there. He walked through the night and made his way through rough terrain. Past torn apart buildings, empty burnt-out cars and makeshift gravestones for miles to see.

He slept little, ate less. But knew it wouldn't be long before he would get his next task. These were desperate times and a killer is as a killer does.

Sweating and tired, he had been walking for two days and needed water when he spotted a small local trader spot on the side of the road. He was desperate for anything to quench his thirst. The foul tastes he's gotten used to would suffice, no matter how rancid, and the murky water he bought was no different. Out here Dante often had to rely on roots, animals with growths and things one would hardly mention as a food source. Long stretches of open roads, with little promise of water lay ahead. Dante would have to walk at least two days to get to the next town or outpost.

This town was bigger than the first, the former town of Beaufort West. It was in the early 2000's it changed to a mining town, where a Russian private firm bought over the rights of previous abandoned mines. What was known as a friendly sheep country was changed to a mining landscape for the greedy, who sat safely far away whilst the land was plundered. People objected, but were silenced promptly. The scarce water resource in this district was not helped by the large consuming mines. It was known for little rainfall, but had well-known rich resources of underground water that was at risk from contamination. The company moved in fast, and built an infrastructure. Chinese immigrants flocked to the town to help build big infrastructures and high rise buildings unlike anyone had seen before. It was the modern Wild West, but this time spreading through South Africa. New embassies and air routes were opened. On the continent new Chinese and Russian elites were seen everywhere, with ties right to the top of Government. They built expensive mansions and drove fancy cars. Their children went to private schools and ate the finest foods. Better roads were built, and soon the local shops were replaced by markets filled with cheap Chinese goods. The Railways that the government of Apartheid built was extended, linking to the ports, making way for uranium transports that was placed on boats traveling to China. Intercontinental Roads became a relative mandate and practice. Cultural centers sprung up across the towns and even schools brought in Mandarin; Cantonese and Russian as compulsory languages. The original population of Beaufort West by could by this stage not do much to fight the changes and it seemed to be for the better of everyone. There were work oppor-tunities, bursaries for children and safety. All for trading their way of life... It was a prosperous time that would end in heart-ache. Poor practices of environmental watch, and officers being bribed all soon led to malpractice. Strong winds would blow over the mines and with it blew radiated particles, dumped in bags, often left open and poorly discarded. It was a health risk at large, people inhaled it, ingested it, absorbed it through the skin and let it become part of them. The promises of rehabilitation of the lands were mere words. The mines responded by saying it was not in the business of rehabilitation and would not follow such a path.

The corporations dug deeper into the earth in search of uranium. As predicted the plants started to show symptoms of radiation sickness. Food became more scarce and crude as the lowest forms of life were mashed into packs of sustenance. The gusts of radiated winds blew over the schools, infecting the children with the most horrendous sickness. Cancer became citizen and the radiated waves of air populated the towns as they kept digging deeper.

People would drop dead in the streets and be swiftly removed in order to keep a jagged sense of order in the growing chaos. Soon, the town was left in disarray. The Government pulled out and left the survivors to their doom.

As Dante walked into the town he recalled memories of this place and his youth. He spent a few years here, staying with his uncle as a child, before he was taken in by the military. Most of the memories were a blur by now, only mental pictures. He walked past an old processor which crushed uranium ore from the shafts. A wasteland of hazardous radioactive material was left behind, now the playground of scavengers and those who had nowhere else to go. The wide streets with old historic buildings, and large towers stood mostly abandoned, slowly becoming derelict. People wandered around meaninglessly, without hope.

Standing on top of a pile of rubble, a man with a husky voice shouts to a small crowd like a mad man, he seems desperate. Dante walks closer trying to avoid unwanted attention or getting noticed. No one here has seen him since he was a child, but Dante can still recall their chants for his blood. He couldn't risk getting noticed, lest he have the military informed about his whereabouts. As far as he knew no one in the military knew he was alive, he had to tread carefully. Here you'd be sold out to the military for a packet of smokes. The thick rag served multiple purposes apart from obscuring his face. Disease spread around these type of towns like wildfire, and with little or no medicine, people stayed sick for months, dying from simple flu.

The man was still shouting to the crowd, his words difficult to understand. He spoke with a thick Northern Cape accent, uttering words that Dante understood, mixed with a Griqua Afrikaans vernacular. His plead was clear. He had with him 2 canisters, big holders with what appeared to be clear water, the source, unknown. He offered this luxurious resource to anyone who could bring back his love. Slowly the crowd took interest, the tension boiling. Crowds of this size were hotpots for violence. It was uncertain if he was to be killed by the crowd, water taken and left to return to earth but they were listening closely, observing.

The Griqua man showed no sign of weakness, even though he was clearly in need of help. He was standing proud, the descendant of an old African tribe. The woman he loves had been taken that night, his young son left murdered in the sand. The man returned to the town to find nothing but blood in the room and one clue that made it clear to him who took her. It seemed from the mess that there was a struggle. His boy was young, but brave, a true Griqua by heart. He asked his son to look after his mother while he was away. Little did he know that his departure would cost more than he would bring back from his trade.

Dante carefully gathered information from Dwellers. Drunkards and Dwellers have a reputation for having loose lips."Doesn't hurt to have a blade firmly pressed on their carotid arteries" Dante thought to himself. In these towns, there were rumors, stories of a creature known in the old days as the Tokoloshe. A water sprite often described as a brown dwarf like creature. The Griqua man, named Lindley, told Dante all he knew hoping this info could bring his lover back somehow. Close to the town border was the old Ryst Kuil mine. It was said that the creature stayed there. People did not enter this abandoned mine for years, why would they even risk it? The shaft had various sinkholes, parts where the mining shafts were falling in. Dante was not a superstitious man. If this man wanted to give him water to dispose of this supposed demon, bring back his woman, then that is what it will be. Dante walked towards the old mine, the gates barely standing and rusted beyond the point of re-use, burnt wire showed signs of traders who melted old telephone and electric cables. Copper was still a valuable resource to be traded. A radioactive sign, the yellow paint peeling off, hangs by its rusty hinges on the gate. Dante stayed outside the mine examining the grounds for movement, looking for traps and the best way in. Dante waited for nightfall before moving in. It was a full moon. Dante walked in slowly, careful noting the signs of rot. The last thing he wanted was to get caught in a cave in. No one would search for him. Out here, he was on his own. Carefully taking his steps, using a solar power charged LED light he carried with him. This instrument was one of the few that Dante still had with him from the military. The tunnels showed what was once a glorious rich mining operation, but decay over the years made this place a forgotten museum. Instruments left in the tunnels, all relics. The air became more dense and warm as Dante walked deeper down the shaft. A strange sound drew Dante deeper in, what sounded like an old hymn being sung. Deeper Dante went, following the voice.

Dante climbs up through a narrow passage with a rope that moves up. The space is dark, and at some parts difficult to imagine anyone would be staying down here. Turning back was a good option. Building a rep as a bounty hunter meant finishing the task. It became clear from the fresh footsteps that who or whatever was in here was not far. Down the dark passage, Dante could see a refuge chamber, one of the finest last designs implemented to the mines. They were built to be able to have an indefinite supply of breathable air and power, one of the prime inventions created before the fall, to help them go deeper, into the darkest earth soil. By the looks of it, it was still operational. The underground passage was warm, unbearable as Dante moved further, but close to the refuge room he could feel a fresh breeze of air. Dante noted a deep dark hole, just past the refuge room and in the corner of his eyes he saw a strange figure humming the song. The Tokoloshe… A man, covered in dirt, by the looks of it he had been injured in a blast accident. The side of his face burnt, with growths covering his open arm. The creature sat humming a song whilst holding onto a long rope, stretching down a narrow hole.

From time to time he looked down shining a light. A voice could be heard, the voice of a woman. He pulled the rope up slowly and out of the dark comes a young Griqua woman. She fit the description Lindley gave. She was short in stature, with emerald green eyes. Her arms bruised by going down the small cave to some underground stream. She sat inside a big bucket, hoisted down and pulled up by a pulley system, one of the primitive designs of miners. As she gets to the top she sheepishly hands over small containers filled with water. It was clear that he found something very precious, but it was obviously too dangerous to go down there himself. The ground shakes and dust fills the air. Possibly underground passages, the earth is slowly claiming back. The screaming of the woman could be heard, irritating the creature. He smacks her through the face in annoyance. A tear rolls down her bruised cheek. The creature looks down at his gift, bottles of fresh water. He drinks, gulping down like a drowning fish. His face deformed. No wonder he retracted to the darkness, luring in the weak to keep him alive. The heat was beating down on Dante and he knew he had little time. The moist walls made slippery tracks of the rock formations. Dante sneaks closer, coming up behind the Tokoloshe.

The creature was not aware of Dante as he gulped down his water. Empty cans of preserved food were lying around. Dante tread carefully around it, drawing the blade on his side. The woman sees the shadow but before she could make a sound Dante strikes, jamming the blade square into the beast's skull. Blood gushes out. The little beast looks to his side and drops to his knees as Dante pulls out the blade. He struggles to crawl away, eyes beginning to bleed as he makes sounds similar to a dying cat. The woman, fearful of who Dante is moves away, grabbing onto an old mining instrument in self-defense. The dying creature looks up at his murderer. His eyes seem familiar to Dante. The creature tries to cover his head, his body weak, mumbling words. At first unclear… The Tokoloshe's eyes widen as he looks up at Dante.

"Dante." he murmurs.

His hand stretches out towards Dante as he drops to the floor. His can of water spills over the floor mixing with blood. Dante mindfully look around to see if there is anyone else around. He slowly walks closer to see if the little beast was surely dead. Dante tries to speak to and move closer, but the woman was still traumatized by all she had been through and kept moving away with every step Dante took. Understandable really, everyone cracks under the pressure eventually. Dante tries to remember who this creature that uttered his name was. Back in the military they were taught by their recollection officer, very elaborate ways of remembering, as a tool to recollect info from scenes they came about. During the training, Dante recalled early childhood memories, pictures so clear that it felt real as he saw it. These were known as sparks. Dante had stopped exploring his own past long ago, the sparks served no real purpose he felt, always keeping his attention on the now. Dante places his hand in his pocket and takes out an object. Displaying it to the woman, it was a ring made from an old South African R5 coin with Mandela on the side, melted and bent to form a broad ring. She knew Lindley wouldn't give it to anyone. She skittishly moves to Dante's side, still holding onto her ring. The woman takes a few of the bottles, giving some to Dante. Dante slowly moves out from the space, through the narrow mining passages, the woman close by his side. As they move out Dante could feel the air changing. Thinking back to the Tokoloshe's face, scarred from the environment, drawn back into the mines for a chance to survive. His face melted beyond recognition. Dante tries to figure out how he could recognize him, and who he was. No Tokoloshe that was for sure. Rather a man using small women to bring out water from this resource. Dante knew in the wrong hands this resource would soon become a battle zone. It was best left undiscovered. Dante looked around as they walked out, the sun sitting on the horizon. The emerald green eyes of the woman shone in this light, a strange sense of hope still shining through.

Dante brought back the woman to her husband in the early hours of the evening. He was careful to make sure others did not see them. The man Lindley had a quiet way about him. Seeing his love returned he placed his arms around her holding onto her, no words were needed. They were careful about their water usage, even though she was wounded on her arms from her ordeal in the mines. The man carefully dressed her wounds using minimal water, and some herbal mixture that he kept in a jar. On his arm the man had a tattoo, a symbol of a time before this, of a man known as Adam Kok. The man was a great leader to the Griqua people, uniting them after disputes with the British and Boer, helping them to move towards their own land later known as

Griqualand East. This was however a short-lived victory. Talking through the night, revealed to Dante that Lindley was a direct descendant of this leader. The Griqua now were a tribe with a troubled fate and no land to hold onto as a home. Dante knew that he couldn't stay in this town, but from the short time he spent with these two people he had the feeling they would be the best keepers of the water resource. Filling his containers with water, Dante stayed over for the night after insistence, making for him the best meal they could with what little they had. They had no information of use relating to the Cape Rebels, or of any military movement. They insisted that Dante could take whatever he needed, that he could start a life in this town and that they would help him where they could. But staying in a single place would be dangerous to Dante. For all he knew the military had sent scouts, even Blood Brothers to find him, or evidence of his death. It was not custom for anyone to leave the military, alive at least.

Dante saw many men carry their grievances, hiding their questions as they served, but none really had anywhere else to go. The world was scarred, starving and violent. Dante knew he still needed to learn much of this world. He needed to become a better survivor. He did not want to be recognized again. Dante asked the woman one request. He was very specific in this and requested a change of clothes, something that would serve the purpose of his new task. The woman did not spare any time in making this outfit. This stranger saved her life. She would return the favor. She started off with a hood to cover his head against blazing desert sun, made from a dark and heavy material that would last in the scorching desert, pieces of his old armor sewn into it for added protection.

Dante explained to them how this water resource can give them and their people a chance to a new start, but that it was dangerous, they had to be careful. Before the sun rose, Dante set out to uncharted plains, in search of more information of the Cape Rebels. It didn't take long for word to spread and Dante was called upon, quest after quest ranging from retrieval to murder.

Dante did not get involved with choosing the right from the wrong.

It was merely survival, making friends and foes as he went along.

It was a dangerous way of living but the only way Dante could see

any sense of a hopeful future.

8

Hopeful Inclinations

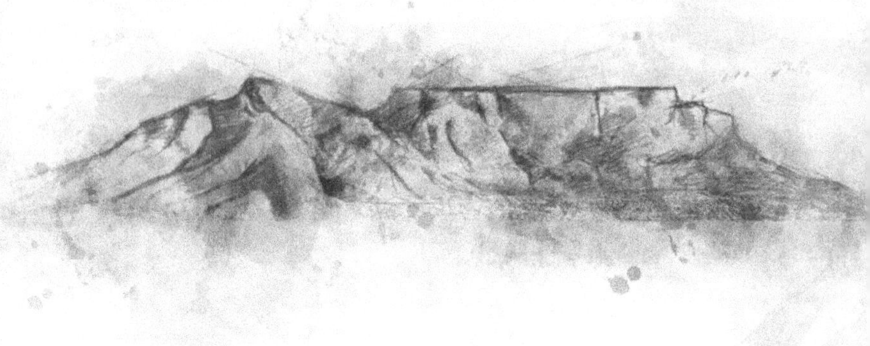

The place was large, stocked shelf to shelf with all things robotic. Anything from old televisions to computer screens. Everything imaginable was in there. There were miniature little robots sitting all over the place and half built others waiting to be finished. The place was tidy as could be. Dante was lying unconscious in a helicopter pilot seat, another relic of a time before this. The space seemed to be alive with all the electronics, surveillance cameras, electronic toys and bits and pieces collected and rebuilt to have new functions. Electric cables hanging from the ceiling to a battery pack, a source of power running from the top to a solar panel. A Muslim man named Zahir was busy tinkering at his workstation close to where Dante was passed out. The same man whom Dante saw earlier tied to a pole and left for dead. The man dragged Dante into this place, fascinated with his robotic arm, a testament of the military's latest technological advancements. He would have loved to explore it in more detail, but there were more pressing matters to attend to. Dante was unsure where he was as he opened his eyes, still feeling woozy from the food poisoning the light slightly stinging his eyes as he squinted around.

"Wakey, wakey." said Zahir.

Dante opened his eyes, looking around him. Dante tries to get up, stumbling over his own feet. Zahir helps him up and places him back in the chair.

"You step with the grace of a drunken Gazelle, stranger." Zahir said with a wide grin on his face."I understand that you are con-fused. The beans… I use it to get back at them. Severe food poisoning, sorry... I found you lying unconscious in the sand, so I brought you here."

Dante looks around, still feeling sick and woozy his skin pale and beaded in sweat.

"Where am I?" ask Dante, standing up on shaky feet.

"I need your help." replied Zahir.

Dante looked straight at Zahir.

"You poison me. Kidnap me and now you want my help? Forgive me, but I'm not familiar with this form of hospitality."

There was a moment of silence between them as Dante let his eyes wonder around this burial ground of electronics.

"Accidental poisoning... And now I'm helping you get better. Quid pro Quo Mr. Dante... I help you, and you help me..." said Zahir.

They both stared at each other.

"The men you are looking for, I know where they are. They took my son, Aziz. I would do anything to save him, but I am not a fighter, you are." Zahir seems to be a desperate man, but very persistent about this request, his eyes fixed on Dante.

Dante lifts up a piece of metal.

"What can you offer me? All you have is crap." answer Dante.

Zahir takes the metal and places it back down carefully against the wall behind him.

"I am not a wealthy man, but there is something of great value of yours I have, the ancient flower. I will give it back to you, only if you help me save my son."

"You want to pay me, with my own possessions?" ask Dante.

Zahir looks at Dante and realizes he does not even know the value of what he has been carrying along with him. How such an important plant could be hidden for so long, and that it survived!

"You don't know anything about what you carry, do you? This could be the means to salvation, for all of us. Do you understand?" ask Zahir.

Dante was getting irritated on top of still feeling dizzy. He had no time for games.

"Salvation!!! Do I look like a Saviour to you?" questions Dante impetuously.

"Get my boy back first. Then I will show you the great importance you so obviously toss aside." answer Zahir.

Dante searches for his sword, and the side blade he keeps hidden. Taken... Zahir slowly moves down to his knees.

"Please. I beg you as a humble man and a father. Save my boy. You are a man of honor. I see it in your eyes. These evil things you do, the killings… They do not define who you are. That choice is reserved for you alone!" pleads Zahir.

Dante contemplates a bit as Zahir rises from the floor and hands him his gear including his sword and what little water he had left. If the legends were true about this man, his boy would have a chance to survive, even against the men who captured his boy.

"This world of ours was beautiful once. We saw to it that this beauty became spoiled and corrupt. But there is still good, we can't afford to lose what little of that we have left". Zahir says somberly.

Dante feels taken aback. It was always a gamble and one needs to be willing to risk the price to play, to survive to see another day. His son meant everything to Zahir.

"Please help me. And I will help you. I promise. My word is my bond." Zahir pleads again.

Dante nods.

"Do we have a deal?" asks Zahir eagerly at this gesture.

Dante looks down at the hand held out to him and shake hands with Zahir. Making deals were no strange manner for Dante. The Devil would always get his due within every Faustian trade Dante engaged in. It was all the same. It was a matter of mutual interest, a pure trade, and when the deal was over their paths would split into different directions. Dante had a feeling that the task would not be as simple as it seems though, it never was. Zahir started gathering his things. He put a robotic dinosaur in his bag and quickly gathered a few other things. Dante watched him gather his things. The warm sun struck Dante as they walked out of the bunker room. The sun has not been kind for years. Didn't help Dante much that he had been poisoned recently. The sun beat down on his head. The land stretched out wide with no person in sight. The heat danced in waves off the horizon. Dante knew that even though this land was barren, danger could be hiding anywhere. Whether scavengers or cannibals. Dante was still woozy from the poisoned beans, but he needed the protea back for some reason, for a silly promise he made to someone he barely knew, but that changed all he ever knew. He also needed to get Sam. The bounty on his head was well worth it. The stories around this man didn't mean anything to Dante, he was just another target. If there was a better offer for someone else, he would gladly take it. The world was no place for heroes, only survivors.

Zahir was smiling, practically whistling a tune as they walked through the different terrains and zones. There was a strange deter-mination to his face, but it could also be pretend, trying to hide behind his fear for what is to come. Dante has seen all kinds of fear through the years, and the worst of what created the fears in people, often his target for a bounty. Rumors became mere trophies, a way to water. The rumors spread far and wide. Zahir took basic supplies for their trek across the barren land. The wind was silent, dying down and carried an ominous tune. When the sun is in full blaze with the wind it was like rough sandpaper on skin. A quiet moment before everything goes wrong, a calm before the storm. A sand dune sloped and curved across a barren land. The sun frying down, scorching anything it touched, a black ashen skeleton is an exception to that. Bone is not prone to being boiled. The two figures lay hidden in the sand, a camouflaged tarp serving to hide and protect them from the suns' heat. Dante and Zahir lay hidden underneath, spying on the nearby factory down the hill. Dante looked through a weathered rifle scope and saw enough for him to already have worked out a plan of infiltration in his head, a side effect of military training, thoughts in process. Down the hill there was no sign of life or activity, no evidence, nothing but the massive carcass of the factory. Its decrepit form gives no hint to what purpose it might have served but if Zahir was right, then like Dante, this building found a second destiny when the world was destroyed.

"You sure they're there?" ask Dante.

"They are down there. They need several in-between hideouts to refill on ice otherwise the organs don't keep the journey." Zahir answers him with assurance.

A hidden trail snaked along the side of the dunes, the wind was strong there. The weather in the Cape was unpredictable, now more so than ever. Long ago an earthquake shook out of the earth and raised the sea. Now beaches tower while cities crumble to the depths. Zahir was leading Dante through the sandy trail. Zahir's steps trampled with familiarity, he had been here before.

"The Cape Frontier has been in a severe clash with the Commandos in the North. So, they have been staying away from the Karoo." says Zahir.

Dante returns to earth and follow discreetly behind Zahir.

"That's good for northern borders but it means these people can do what they want out here. I've heard rumors that the Frontiers' resources aren't doing so well either." says Dante. Dante's thoughts fly over the broken waters of the Ocean. Dante was indeed a weary man. He was born into this world bearing upon his shoulders the problems of others. Eventually they crushed the little boy into coal and this hunk of coal over time formed into a rough diamond, a blood diamond. So red in fact that from far it would appear pitch black, but upon close inspection would be a concentrated crimson. The wind dies down ending the stream of sand upon the march.

9

On Broken Wings
and Empty Prayers

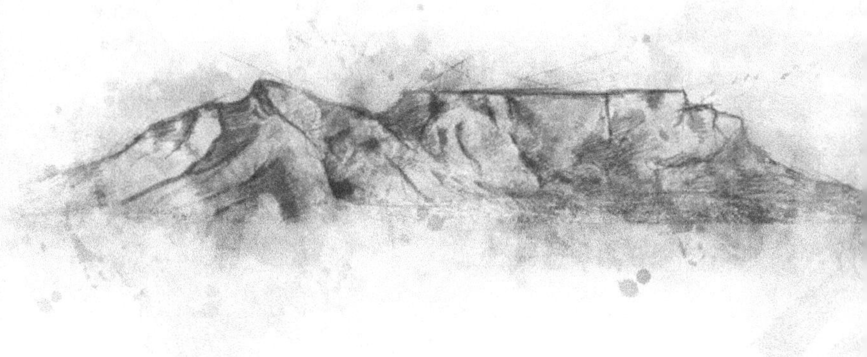

omewhere in his nightmares Zahir has been here. The smell of blood caress his nostrils, bleach and decay hang thick in the air. This was no place for people to be, none living anyway. Those who listened closely could hear the ghosts of the past, on the fringes of his Zahir could sense them lingering. Torn open corpses, hanging about in the air watching him and Dante approach the factory. Eyeless sockets that echoes their morbid drones to turn back, to go away. A chill went down Zahir's spine leaving him in a cold sweat and his legs began to shake. Demons were near and he wasn't sure he was strong enough to face them. But Zahir would do anything for his son. Even risk the gates of hell. They make it to the side of the factory. Its ruin cast a massive shadow over the two. Dry blood caked the walls. Still they heard nobody close by and they continued cautiously through a screen door near the far corners. Dante readied his blade and used it to feel out before him. Zahir close behind, afraid, shivering beneath his layers of clothing. They entered the factory and were immediately greeted by a massive swarm of flies like a black veil of buzzing little creatures. The flies ate better than people did, buzzing around rotted, open corpses streaming with maggots. There were bodies of men, women and children. They lay face down, Zahir searched for his son. Relief washed over him as he realized Aziz was not lying there. Dante's grip tightened around the hilt of his sword. He couldn't wait to decapitate whoever was responsible. It wouldn't be murder, but justice. That was his favorite part about his occupation, killing. For once he would really enjoy the kill, because someone who did this did not deserve to live. It was like putting down a rabid mutt. Dante methodically placed his silent steps with his primed blade leading the way. Zahir noticed the grace with which the bounty hunter moved. Dante's mind was quiet, for he had a monster on which he could rely on, a demon of his own. A demon, that awoke when he was very young. The factory was coated with a dark atmosphere and smelt of rot. Trails of blood smeared across the floor up to the large factory door, most probably where they drag the bodies through. There was a light far away in the corner, a crack in the sheet metal allowing a shard of light to filter through, illuminating the nearby area and catching Dante's eye. A figure appeared and cut out the light just briefly before disappearing into the murk. And then a scream so loud it echoed through the factory walls and shook the windows.

The figure cuts the light again, seeming to move in their direction. Dante hides and drags Zahir with him underneath a long metal shelf rusted over the years. In fact, the entire place was coated in brown fungal rust but the dark made it difficult to discern between what was rust and what was dried blood. The shrieks of misery persisted again cutting in and out with repetitions of mere seconds in between, temporal bird like shrieks. He crawls forward to get a closer look, intrigued by the conductor of this symphony of misery. Moving closer to the light, he sees a man with a leather plague-mask on. And it finally made sense to

Dante what this place had become. This was where people were brought to be recycled, a crude food processing plant, an abattoir full of human cattle. From the dark, Dante and Zahir spy on the masked man, tracking his movements.

The Doctor, Peter gathered his bucket of rust covered tools, most of them not even medical tools and the others were horrifyingly so. He was a brutish man, built like a farmer. His fore-arms called to mind a certain crusty; spinach loving sailor and his belly was bulbous, a combination of sinuous muscle and hardened fat. He was swathed in blood and gore from head to toe. Peter hated it when they passed out. He found the place too quiet after all that screeching. He heard a noise and went to go investigate it. This was his life. He reveled in his butchery. He never showed mercy to anyone. He heard it again, a noise. He felt someone was here. Peter knew how to breathe through the mask. He had grown accustomed to it. The mask was bird like, made by scraps of leather that was once human skin and crudely sewn together.

Dante knew this was no ordinary murderer, not if you look at the meticulous cuts, this was a skilled killer. Dante saw the masked man disappear into a doorway and slowly walks forward. As Dante looks around the corner, the dark figure of the doctor comes out of another doorway close behind him, a tranquilizer gun in hand. Dante walks out of the room and finds himself face to face with the ghost everyone spoke of. He smiles crookedly before shooting Dante in the chest with the tranquilizer. Dante looks down at the needle in his skin and crumples to the floor. Darkness sucks him in, the world starting to swirl once again. Peter chuckles gleefully. He had done what no one else had been able to do. He had caught the red caped bounty hunter. He would enjoy this kill more than any other. Dante attempts to push himself up off the ground, but his muscles have gone limp. He tries to reach his blade with his robotic arm but loses consciousness.

Dante wakes up on the operating table, strapped down as the Doctor looks at him wearing a plastic coat covered in blood. Dante takes a deep breath, he had been in tight squeezes before, but this one was pretty tight. He had to play it cool, psycho's thrived on fear, 'Got off' on terror.

"I heard stories about you. A famous Bounty Hunter, saving lives of so many yet killing even more." Peter picks up a tool and looks at Dante through the mask.

"The Red Cape… That's what gave you away." Says Peter.

"You don't say." reply Dante.

Peter takes his mask off, not reacting to Dante. Dante looks around to see what he can do.

"I never imagined I'd get to meet you, though. The man with a steel arm! The Cut-Throat King! God, I idolize you. The shit they say you did. Beautiful! Operatic in scale. You're a born killer. Just. Like. Me!" Hisses Peter

"I myself saved the lives of some at the expense of others. I used to be a Surgeon at the concentration camps. In the Common-wealth of Virginia and I don't say commonwealth lightly. Then I came to this pretty little Country of yours before it got blown way the fuck up to high Hell, but the Camps here are more to my liking…" says Peter picking up a larger scalpel.

"They never really prepare you for surgery in a war zone. You'd treat a man for a gunshot all the while he was dying of

Tuberculosis. Sometimes I had to take shoe laces and use them to sew up the poor screaming SOB's. Never had a survivor... They were weak. Vermin..." Peter leans down with his knife towards Dante's chest.

"And then shit hit the fan all the way through Sunday. It got pointless. They… were pointless. I wasn't really saving anyone." says Peter, the blade touching Dante's skin"Careful with that. You could cut yourself." taunts Dante.

Dante tries to buy time, unsure where Aziz or Zahir could be.

"And now I save many more lives than before, by selling organs to the needy and food to the hungry." Continue Peter. Peter moves the blade towards Dante's head and holds it to his eye.

"And again, just like me, because of what you do. You have got a lot of enemies."

Peter is excited now, pure giddiness rushes over his face. Blood drips to the floor from his last kill. A corpse is lying on the floor with his entrails strewn everywhere. By the looks of it, seems to have been a rush job, his organs cut out while the man was still alive. The last look of pure pain still etched on his face.

"Many a folk are ready to pay a lot for your head and I am more than willing to deliver." states Peter.

He looks around the room, gore littering the walls.

"The good news is I'll save your organs which may have a long and happy life in the body of the highest bidder. But we don't have time to waste. I am going to start."

The light suddenly goes off. Peter takes off his mask and looks around the room.

"Damn generator." he mumbles.

He looks at Dante and walk out. Peter goes into the next room avoiding the bodies lying on the floor. He walks towards the generator and touches the switch. Suddenly a jolt of electricity passes through him and he shakes and passes out.

———

Peter wakes up tied to the bed, Dante and Zahir standing above him. His coat is off and he is in his white shirt lying on the same bed his victims laid in. Dante takes the plague mask and puts it on the dead victim behind him.

"I was thinking about it and you're right, we are similar in a way." says Dante.

Dante smiles and look at Zahir.

"But unlike you, I have an assistant. I won't let you suffer for too long…"

Zahir walks around to the other side of Peter. Dante's blade mere inches away from Peters face.

"Lucky devil." states Zahir with disdain.

"We are looking for Sam, there is a little boy with them, called Aziz, where are they?" questions Dante.

Peter smiled at them and opens his mouth as if to speak. Dante did not expect Peter to start singing though. With his robotic arm, Dante backhands Peter across the face with such force that teeth fly from his mouth. Dante moves the knife across Peter's eyes then towards his ear."You know, I actually know a spot behind the ear. Make many a man sing a different tune." Dante pushes the point of the knife down hard and a thin trail of blood trickles out.

"If you don't co-operate…"

Peter screams in pain.

"Tropical Sands Hotel! Wednesday night at 8. Sam will be there to trade organs and the boy. The boy is one of the slaves." says Peter.

Dante smiles and pull the knife away.

"We need to hurry, we need to find Aziz." Shouts Zahir.

Zahir looks at Peter, not sure what is going to happen to him.

"We leave him here, if he told the truth… Well he better have. Otherwise I will come back and finish the job." replies Dante.

Zahir picks up his bag and hurries out the door.

"Don't forget your bag." calls Zahir as he exits.

"Just one more question. Who put a bounty out on my head? Was it Rico, Anton, Juan?"

At the last name, Peter's eyes light up. Dante grimaced.

"Juan. Ok." states Dante with a finality that meant death for that man.

Dante picks up his bag and walks out of the room. Peter looks around, and with blood dripping out of his ear, begin singing his song again in a whimper.

10

Silence So Long
within the
Black Oblivion

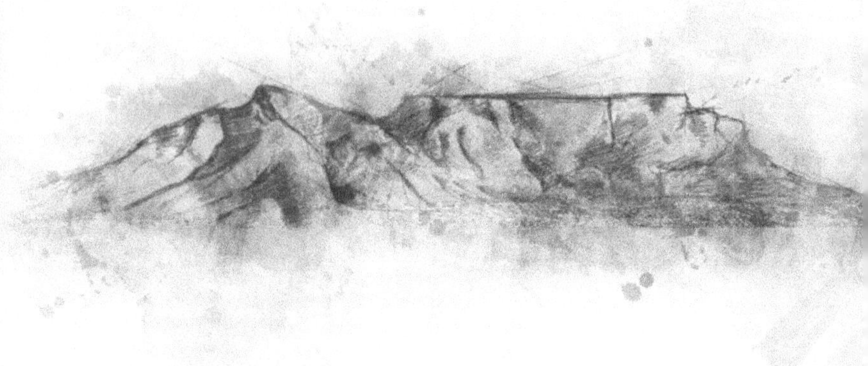

The sun was dipping into the ocean just as Philip was nearing the designated meeting spot. He was making his way to meet the rest of the band, who were waiting for him on the deserted beach about a kilometer from the hotel. They too were watching the golden-red sun slowly vanishing behind the immense horizon. Everyone was captivated by the sight. It conjured a morbid feeling between them as if the sun would never rise again. That it would leave them like an ex-lover. But what it really was, was fear. Fear of the unknown, of all the unknowns in the past, present and future. When night time came, it brought with it a veil of the blackest velvet, and no stars were seen on this night, or all the nights to come. The dark would conjure up visions of the most hellish degree, the worst possible nightmare with eyes wide open. The thought was clear to all who could still draw breath. None were safe. Every living thing in this wretched place wanted to rob, plunder; rape; eat and murder you. You would be lucky to die quickly if these demons were ever encountered. Tonight, something was lurking in the black, something they could not imagine.

Philip met up with the rest of his tribesman, the sabotage scouting troop, and as the sun vanished below the horizon, they all lit their lanterns and continued onward, led by amber light, toward the meeting spot. The wind had picked up with the coming darkness and was howling violently like a hungry wolf. They had reached the abandoned hotel and secured the doorway before entering and setting up camp. The Tropical Sands Hotel was once a five-star resort and prestige holiday destination. Now it was only an empty husk that was slowly sinking into the sand over the passage of time. The hotel had lost the warmth it once had and instead greeted the group with a bitter cold ambience. Despite the fiery brightness exuding from the fire sticks the dark of the dead hotel still seemed to consume it. The lanterns' light would dance off the walls without regard of choreography. Sam and Jenny walked in, making themselves known. Sam greeted Philip and gestured to see the goods. Philip quickly jumped to it, swinging around the hard-cased Camo sack. He flips the locks open letting out a cloud of white ice to greet Uncle Sam's face. Sam reaches in to feel the goods. The organs are soft to Sam's surprise. He signs with his hands"How fresh?" Philip flips and signs with his hands back at the mute Uncle Sam,"Fresh". Sam breaks out into a proud smile and gives the group leader a pat on the back that almost knocked his lungs loose. The meeting room was on the highest floor of the ghostly hotel. Faded wallpaper curled over and shook with the passing wind which came through several gaping holes in the walls. A moldy floor mattress which immediately imposed its subtle stench as the group entered the room. In the middle of one wall was a framed photograph of a green vineyard landscape that was in good condition save for layer of dust on the surface. The photograph elicited in Phillip an envious boil that saw him knock the photograph off the wall. Above them, the roof was half torn apart exposing crisscrossing wooden beams. The place was hollow, no love was here. And the hole in the roof suggested that a gigantic bird could fly by and pluck you right out of there. The group secured the room, careful to lock down every blind spot and assess any possible escape routes. They were ready for anything. After checking the windows and entrances they all met with Sam who took all the torches and lit the overhanging lamp that meant the deal was on. If you were far away, the hotel room would look like a dark block of cement with a star of light flickering inside. The group took up positions ready for whatever was going to come through, each in tactical positions that gave them a complete view and firing access in the room.

Dante and Zahir saw the light coming from the tower. Zahir was smiling, eager to get his boy back. He had in him a new determination. He followed Dante to a lookout tower where one young man stood guard. Inside were small children, chained to the walls. Zahir spotted Aziz right away but Dante stopped him.

"No. Not safe. You wait here, I'll go get your boy back." said Dante walking off.

He drew his sword as he peered into the main door. There were no guards save for one man standing near the children: Juan, the person with a lust for Dante's blood, ready to be slashed into ribbons by Dante's favorite plaything. Juan was screaming at the children. Their faces showing the terror they experienced. With his back turned to the entrance, Dante had a clear advantage over his would-be executioner. He moved silently, begging for the children's silence. When he was close enough, he called to Juan, and swiftly slashed his throat as Juan turned to look around. Never breaking gaze with his would be adversary. The children were terrified, crying and fidgeting in a futile attempt to get away from Dante. Zahir ran into the room and Aziz's face lit up at the sight of his father.

"My boy!" he cried.

"Papa!" shouted Aziz excitedly.

A chain around his fragile neck to keep him in line, Zahir got to work picking the locks of Aziz and then the other children, leaving Dante to walk out with the head of Juan in his hand. Dante walked towards the lit building, towards Sam and cohorts with the intent to slaughter.

Something didn't feel right. Sam looked out of the window and saw the Metalists creeping over the dunes. There were six of them. They were armed to the teeth with guns, knives and bullet proof armor. They had enough weapons to mow down a fair-sized village. And one of them had a flamethrower rig that was belching small blue flames ready to roast if the deal went bad. They all wore signature iron masks of an obsidian color, used to protect, but mostly frighten. They were an intimidating sight, a force straight from the black pits of hell. Just the sight of these metal warriors made Sam feel uneasy. A feeling not mutual to that of his partners'…

Jenny was anxious for something to go down, twitching at the knee. The group seemed too confident, thought Phillip. He was reluctant to show them the goods but they made good on their currency, ten liters of fresh water. The tall Metalist places the clean water down which was housed in a juggernaut sized container that tested the strength of the table legs as it dropped down.

"The organs?" the tall Metalist asks coldly.

His words like bass mumblings under the mask. Phillip looks to Sam unsurely, sensing something wrong with the transaction. Sam studies the Metalist's composure and sizes up the tattooed woman, he had his reservations but you could never tell from the emotionless expression he held.

"It's all legit. The water's clean" she says, eager to make the deal and move on with her cut. Sam's hands sign, and Phillip interprets."Take off the mask." He demands of the large Metalist. The tension flares up between the two as Sam makes his demands.

The mask was their sacred right and represented their spiritual power. Asking a Metalist to remove his mask was a great insult. The metal gimp in anger shot a cloud of flame in the air lighting the room up and stunning the group. He was ready to burn someone. Everyone in the dwelling drew their weapons and aimed it at their mirror counterpart, ready to kill at the drop of a pin, a true Mexican stand-off. One mistake could lead to blood bath. Phillip aimed his dagger at the masked man's heart already calculating in his head an escape route for when the bodies began to fall. He was really itching for a hit. Then suddenly the Tall Man lifted his hands up gesturing to everyone to be calm, but it just made the situation tenser. Then uncharacteristically he slowly removed his mask showing them his honest, unscarred white face. He seems to be freshly shaven and shoots a smile which breaks the tension. He starts laughing making sure to look each and every Sabotage member in the eyes, assuring them it's all good. The Tall Man turned to his over eager friend and gestures for him to stand down. The metal Gimp lowers his flame thrower and with it easing everyone's anxiety. Not wanting to get burnt to a crisp had adverse effects on people's mental health. The group calmed down and was back in business mode. Phillip looked to Sam who gave him a nod of approval, his face in a slight scowl. The standoff had done nothing to change his demeanor.

Finally, they were in business and that was all he cared about, however the showdown was going to end, Sam knew it was going to be a productive night. Phillip swung the Camo bag on the table and flipped it open, the masked man and tattooed woman leaning over slightly. A cloud of dry ice smoke wisps up to greet their cheeks. The tattooed woman reached in and poked the fleshy cargo, very surprised at the freshness.

"Damn these are fresh." stated the woman.

"O positive as requested, heart and liver, all intact. Will match your candidate anytime." answered Phillip.

The tattooed woman was wholly impressed.

"It checks out, give them the water." replied the woman.

A loud thud calls everyone's attention as a fairly large object hits the canister, then the floor. Phillip picks it up, a human head. Turning it around, he sees a familiar nose, a familiar mouth, and familiar eyes. It was Juan. Phillip snaps at the assumed betrayal and launches his dagger into the gimp's chest, dropping him to the floor. It was hell. The Tall Man put his mask back on and opened fire with the rest of the Metalist crew, mowing down the opposition. He flips the table over as cover. Not realizing Phillip grabbed the organs and bolted out of the window with a ghostly swiftness from the other side. No one noticing Dante crouched in the darkness on the roof. Phillip reached the outskirts of the hotel and was going to make a dash for the beach to escape this slaughterhouse. He stopped to look for Sam, who rolls down the steps with Jenny ahead as they make it out. Suddenly Dante comes from the side and slams into Phillip. Stunned and a bit shaken he jumps aside and draws his garden shear weapons in hand. They clash their blades in the darkness on the soft beach sand. Dancing around each other like wild mongrel mutts over a scrap of rotting meat. Phillip was tired. Too tired to see Dante jam his blade into his chest and out his back, cutting his life short.

But Sam was long gone and the triumph he should feel is gone.

He walks out of the building into the darkness.

11

Nothing Good Lasts

Zahir freed all the children, including his son, but knows it isn't safe for them. He holds Aziz's hand tightly and they make a run for it. They run with the others across the dunes and away from the evil of this place. He smiles at his son, tears of joy in his eyes. Then he feels it. The bullet's impact knocks him off his feet, killing him instantly. It was so sudden, that Aziz's delayed reaction only hardened the emotional blow. He cries out kneeling down by his father, the dead body lying in the sand, blood pouring out of the wound. Aziz rolls his father over.

"Papa, Papa!" he cried

A figure looms above him and he looks up to see the glimmer

of a robotic arm. The man kneels down and looks at Zahir. Aziz knows this man saved their life. He looks at the man."Wait, my father wanted me to give you this." said Aziz taking out a robotic toy and pulling out the protea out of a secret compartment. Dante takes it, holds it tight, and walks away.

Sam and Jenny watched from far away, and saw Phillip's corpse in the sand. They made their way home, no organs but water was what they had come for. Their friend and brother was dead, a sad loss for all. Sam knew this was a close call. Too close for comfort. His arm stung where the bullet grazed him. If it wasn't for his sharp mind and quick reaction, he'd have been dead. Jenny looked tired, so did he. It was a hard night. It was a long walk home. Halfway home they met up with the boys. One boy, Ezra hung back from the rest.

"Where's Phillip?" he asked.

Jenny shook her head but said nothing. The boys were silent. They would mourn the loss in their own way. Ezra ran off through the darkness towards the hotel, searching for Phillip's body, and finding it easily. He knelt down next to his former mentor. Mourning was replaced by rage. Revenge manifested itself in the cruelest way. He cursed the sky and howled at the moon. He swore a most violent vendetta, an end to the man who wrought this violence…

Dante watched Aziz from afar. He knew what he had brought upon himself. He became an avatar of misery and hatred, everything he fought against. The boy was digging a shallow grave with a rusted number plate. His lips were burnt dry and his skin was bright red and leathery. The hole he dug was for two. Dante didn't know when last he saw a grave being dug for anybody. Back then, when he was a child they'd bury the dead in the crop lands to help them grow. The dead weren't honored anymore. The number plate broke in two and became useless. The boy started using his hands shovel out sand in scoops. Dante watched as the boy dragged the body into the grave and began throwing sand over the body. Dante tucked the protea back in his bag and walked away. Death was not a subtle thing in the wastes. It was the closest thing to God anyone knew. And worship was the simplest thing.

About 100 meters from the burial site, Aziz turned around to give his father a last goodbye. To his dismay he couldn't find the grave exactly. The entire valley was littered with indiscriminate rocks, blending in the marker of his father's grave. All the boy had left now was just memory and prayer. Prayer for a man he loved and so the chant whispered from his lips, floating into the netherworld where he imagined his father was listening.

12

The End
is the
Beginning

The smell of marijuana hung thick in the air. It was 'down time' which meant no good. A day of hard work in the dust deserved its reward they would say. Smuggled and stolen food would be enjoyed... cans of beans, biltong. Sometimes even coffee. Everything enjoyed in excess along a plethora of drugs and alcohol. Various types of music would play over one another. In one corner, the foreboding melancholic gospel and country sound of Johnny Cash would compete over Bauhaus and Marilyn Manson. The chaotic atmosphere would seek to emulate the hellish world outside. This madhouse became the home of Dante. Not for long, however. Dante is busy putting together food for his

Uncle, scraping together what they had left. The room is darkly lit and sparsely decorated, mostly adorned with keepsakes from the outside. Dante overhears a woman screaming, a weekly tradition. The men here had their way with whoever they pleased. Murder was rare, but still an ill fate for the weak ones. The violent way of life succumbed to primitive traditions and practices.

He would crawl away in the nights before the sharp chill would set in and watch the rats scurry from their abysmal holes, feeding on whatever miserable scraps they could find. The boy would just lay there in silence and watch the mutilated rodents with childlike curiosity as they fought each other for nothing but mere bones and rotting sinew. Animals were easy. He had come to admire their survivalist mentality. They were fine-tuned to the horrors and hardships around them. They had learned to stride the lakes of hell and chew on sulphur to live. Purity... Animals were easy to understand. People on the other hand, were cruel and greedy, hateful in their complexity. Envious and fearful of come whatever may. They wanted to live in the"Land of do what you want". Instead they settled for the "Land of take what you please". Hellish Anarchy... Disorder, rape and murder became the inheritance of whatever children still remained, to ponder and comprehend through black and white eyes.

One particularly vile creature was staring the boy down through the barrel of a rusted revolver. The old man was prone to these sadistic games of chance. In his drunken stupors, he'd seek to harm the boy. Harm anything that he saw as 'better off than himself'. Daniel had even come to enjoy the burn of the distilled fuel. He fantasized about it on those long cold nights and unbeknownst to him it was affecting his mental health, filling his brain up with acidic whispers that call for the boys' eyes to be gouged out. By the end of the night Dante was about to learn that fifty percent of any jest is based in truth. His Uncle would try and kill him, wanted to kill him. The boy was setting food on the table as usual. With swift turnings in the dusty shack floor he was checking every hiding place for something fit to be a meal. At this point, anything would do. His uncle was becoming impatient.

The swigs were burning more deeply now, more honestly as the whisper floated up from his stomach, begging for a meal. He readied the table with a scrap of old bread and old newspaper. It was better than nothing at all. Dante went to help his crippled uncle, his pride wounded by the gesture. But his waning strength afforded him no other choice. He took calculated falls with his wooden leg that started just above the knee. It was a crude imitation of a foot and resembled the mass produced passionless skill of its creator. Basic craftsmanship... It was difficult to walk on and at night would cause the man discomfort. He would wake up in the middle of the night and gasp at the pain in the absent leg. A ghost pain...

"Let it go, why don't you go run along and disappear." he snapped.

Dante was used to such spiking jabs, molding him with the sense that he was worthless. The old man clawed down on the boys' shoulder and lowered himself onto the chair. Daniel was a hulk of a man. In his prime he trumped rugby players in frame and power. Now, the muscle turned to fat and the man was a dusty shadow of his former self. Dust that he couldn't clean off for the life of him... The dust covered everything. Every crack and crevice and surrounded all borders of the town on every horizon. It was a silent landlord. After a while nobody bothered to clean it off anymore. They settled for the winds blowing off old dirt and covering them in a fresh film of coarse sand. Daniel tore the paper with his hands and scoffed it down. Using his saliva to lubricate his cancerous throat...

"What's this shit? Lazy, good-for-nothing little gnat you are. Didn't bother catchin' no rats today? Want your Uncle to starve? I clothe you. I put a roof over your flea ridden mug and you don't even bother to provide a decent meal. If I have to look at this mediocre shit again, I'll cut your fuckin' legs off and have myself a feast!" Daniel screamed drunkenly at the boy. Dante looked at the floor, piss running down his pants leg, forming a puddle around his chair.

It was night and that low hum was in the air again, the drunken singing and guffawing of the local miners. Chanting crass lyrics filled with all forms of debaucherous insinuation like the Pirates of the Golden Years. Dante always favoured the night. You could hide better at night. He lay awake on the ground, propping his head up with his arm. Heavy footsteps approached carrying a shadow outside Dante's room. The figure was brooding. Dante heard him but didn't react. It was typical of the old man to brood in the darkness, to watch, to mumble a complaint to himself about the boy, how much of a burden he was. That was all Dante heard, and it was these times he would try to fall asleep, his Uncle's obscenities were his lullaby's. But Daniel didn't come to sing lullabies this night. More sinister thoughts crept in, supplanting rationale and feeding hatred. He stood in the doorway, knife in hand about to do some work. Dante felt something was not right. And with the forward step of the old man, was prompted to awaken and see. Immediately he picked up on the shiny blade through the trickles of light slivers. The boy jumped up and instinctively headed to the corner of the room to get away. Daniel jabbed at Dante, clumsily attempting to slice the boy in his drunken stupor."I took you in." shouted Daniel.

"Gave you a home and all you did was darken my doorway." slurred Daniel.

Daniel was becoming winded from his missing swipes, wheezing loudly.

"Insignificant Insect." he whispered. Daniel cornered the boy and stabbed at him wildly. Howling like a rabid dog. The boy scurried out of the corner and grabbed a nearby fire poker in a futile attempt at defending himself. Daniel felt a cruel sense of enjoyment. Jabbing more wildly at the young boy with the knife like a wild animal. Daniel grabbed at the boy and tossed him against the wall with massive force. Dante bounced off and hit the floor with a dusty thud. He held onto the fire poker for dear life as he struggled to his feet. Daniel stepped forward with his final intent. He was finished playing with his quarry. It was his time to die. A sharp pain shoots its way through his thigh. The cold, burning sensation bringing promises of the most extreme sensation... The boy twisted the object as he pulled it out of his screaming Uncle's pulpy leg and jabbed it into the old man's chest. Harpooning the old fart with quiet rage and hatred... Blood streamed from the open wound in massive excess. His leathery, sweaty face turning a bleak shade of blue and white... In that instant, the cruelty of the world seemed clear to the young boy. As his Uncle lay dying, choking on his own hubris, the boy desperately tried to stop the blood. Killing a man was one thing, but watching the eventual annihilation of a human life would haunt the now fledgling killer.

Dante's hands were drenched in blood, it flowed thick and dark brownish red in colour. He was overtaken by a desperate need that buzzed through his head. Acidic whispers blaming him... He wiped the blood along the dusty floors, covering his hands in a layer of blood and dust. But the blood was dry and it would do nothing to mask his murder. The boy was heaving tears, unable to speak. Only grunts of shame and fear. Dante left the room to vomit. Sounds of people were heard coming closer to their dwelling. Dante saw two shadows of people approaching the door.

"Listen Daniel, we heard you falling around in there again, open up!" a husky smokers voice threatened. Dante was unsure. He scurried on all fours under the table. The men banged hard against the door.

"Boy, tell the old man we're here to collect." another hungry voice threatens.

"Heard you found something of worth today... We know you left early, strange even for you." the man kept banging against the door.

Dante spies the old man's knapsack and pulls it closer. Inside he finds a small amount of gold Kruger coins and clutches them close. Tight and hollow corridors overwhelm him with gossip, all of them seeming to mention the demon boy. He can hear every word of it, every word of their judgmental lather, and until recently he was starting to think they were right. He was a demon. There was nothing he could do to change that fact. A thought insinuated itself that maybe he should start embracing this title of demon, humans disgusted him.

The boy is sitting cuffed in a makeshift office towering with documents and registers. Seated on a salvaged park bench, there was no place but for the small frame of this young boy to sit. His blood and dust caked hand cuffed to the steel armrest, his other bloody hand sitting gently beside him. The boy was lost in thought and remained quiet.

A sturdy military officer walked in, swathed in symbols of rank and achievements from the before time. Meaningless now... The officer, Bennett, was whirling around the fate of this boy in his head. Another lost youth he thought. So common these days... Long had he abandoned the impulse to help the wounded and to save the weak. Years in the Frontier taught him that being good, meant being killed easily. The law of the land was clearer now than ever, die quickly or suffer. He was starting to question that promise as well. Watching Dante through the plate glass brought no sympathy to the Monolithic Soldier. Bennett, a senior officer who joined shortly after the bombs, liked orphaned youngsters of the post war world, entered with an entourage of soldiers and scientists, buzzing with something new to say. Bennett was young but carried himself as a senior. He took a deep breath before trying to explain the absurdity of his report.

"We aren't sure how it happened, but we haven't seen anything like this before." said Bennett.

"People dead, nothing special." stated another officer, brushing him off.

"Three dead, no witnesses... Only the young boy who refuses to speak... He wasn't even heavily armed. I mean, look at him. The townspeople called him a demon child, a devil boy." replied Bennett.

Each picture showing Bennett blood spatters and entrails painted across the modest wooden shack. Such truthful vulnerability, Bennett thought to himself. This boy was gifted and what a gift to have during these uncertain times. Dante turned and looked straight at him as if he could hear their conversation, Bennett smiled. This boy would change his life.

"There was a time that water dripped from the heaven, was abundant in rivers, and you could drink it. But that was a long time ago… before earth took its last breath. The chaos began. Created monsters from the best, devils of the worst… The days are filled with bloodshed, nights with screams of the slain. Desperation tore what remained of our humanity and we are scattered. Searching for hope… Hope is but a distant prayer. Now there is only silence… but not for long."

SHORT STORIES

The following
short stories consists
of how the world came
to be in this state.
The Truth is unknown by now,
a forgotten story.

A tale of meaning
and wonder...
Showing us what could be
if we let it happen.

THE BOOK OF SOL

by David Barbier

Notwithstanding, the life of fire has burned out. The light of the night has burned out. Some souls have been left behind. A fistful of sand tries to grasp but the glass grains trickle down to their brothers. The warm, the constant warm, the fake warm... There is no love here. It is a false perception. We burnt those bridges, severed those ties. An unattainable future drowned in pride and disappointment. A seething torrent washes away juvenile dreams. What dreams we have left are reserved for eat and sleep and protection from the creeps. An exoskeleton of the soul has been absorbed into the earth. The waters reclaim the coastal outlines. The earth shakes like it suffers from epileptic indecision. We have done this. Keep sleeping oh dear world. Do not despair for death is near. Your life is about a droplet in a storm. Nobody dreams anymore. There is nothing to dream about. Like a thief in the night our sleep imaginings were stolen, replaced by evanescent nightmares. Re-living in the days, chasing you into the night... The more connected people were, the more disconnected they became. It's as if I'm trying to forget something. Everything went to hell. We trusted our leaders and were lead straight into these flaming maws. The world was prospering but at the same time was decaying on the inside. Like a golden apple, ripe and ready but as soon as you bite into it, the bitter taste of rot and worms fill your mouth. That day I saw the sun at night and my first thought was that the end is here. Many events can be attributed to the beginning of the end of the information age and of "sane civilisation" but one event could be viewed as the turning point and conversely the symptom that change was on the horizon. It was also a sign that South Africa was about to plummet into the ever-foreboding darkness.

On august 16th 2012 in an area 100km northwest of Johannesburg called Marikana, South African Police opened fire on a crowd of striking mineworkers, injuring 78 and killing 34. These mineworkers were protesting for a wage increase but got more than they could ever bargain for, at least 34 of them did. At the time this tragedy was seen as the most horrific incident of police brutality since the onset of democracy. The event mirrored the memories of brutality suffered under the apartheid security police. Most people don't even have a clue that it happened and others seem to have forgotten. Like there is this sedating fog of the illusion of self-importance. I guess if nothing concerns your general ego why should it matter? But it does and it did. The massacre was the turning point in South African morality. History repeats itself. The earth cycles around the sun, comes back around and replays the topsy-turvy journey. A Cog in a machine blessed to live a predictable course of fate. The more things changed the more they stayed the same. A paradox, but it's this paradox that reflects best the insanity of the situation we found ourselves in. unable to believe the truth because it conflicted with the optimistic hopes. A sedation of self-importance, that my thoughts will overcome the reality of the world.

After the Marikana Massacre was when I began to believe that evil exists in this world, not as a malevolent force out to cause pain but as chaos scrutinized and indulged. Heated disgruntled miners who have been endlessly squashed by the earth and fearful policeman who have been forced to deal with this boiling pot of human anger… And so because of fear, a gunshot added to the chaos which resulted in 34 hardworking South Africans losing their lives in what was supposed to be a fair democratic society. It saddens me to think that all that is left of these miners are only etches on the psyche of those who knew them, like they cease living in the real world and become one of the characters in your head, like your conscience and god. The system failed them. The system broke.

The thing about chaos is that it is contagious. When people become energized by the illusion of truth, they will always rebel against the powers that be. The human machine is not easily definable and it is the very definitions which they altruistically throw themselves at. War is a hungry dog that needs to be fed. It's your responsibility as a sentient creature to impose your will on others before they impose it on you. You have to question a system that can only maintain peace with threat of violence.

But the world moved on, the machine kept pumping and the gears kept spinning and Marikana became all but a thumbprint in the desert sand. These were times of comfortable unrest and people were fighting for more, more than they had, more than they could have wanted, and more than they needed. But it was a necessary fight, one for equality. Years after democracy and the gap between each, people were not imposed by race or gender but by wealth. Soon the fire of protest spread and fevered upon the nationals. At a rally, protesters were arrested. Most of them students and later on they were found executed in cold blood in a nearby field. Must have been intended as an example because people got the message… After that it never took long for general sanity to degrade. War is a drug. It will seduce you with the fire of existential affirmation. And her kiss is fleeting yet sincere. With something to fight for people showed their worth and that worth was gunned down in the street by Chinese supplied weaponry. Cries of equality and freedom became cries of death and regret. South Africa had finally been tainted by the cancer of civil unrest so native to the African continent.

Meanwhile Europe was in crisis. It had found itself in the middle of a conflict between east and west and once the economy of its nations fell, it quickly became a battle ground. Heavy bombings were sustained and the conflict spread like a plague as east and west fought for dominion of the coast. The area was never able to stabilize for a moment's peace, a stalemate of arms, as if east and west were meant to do this forever.

Ocean trades routes became heavily protected and some were even cut off, making it impossible for new supplies to enter the country. This became a problem because civil war was crippling the agricultural industry. Food was running out and water was being stockpiled and controlled by the government. South Africa was also facing major electricity production problems and at the time set out to build a dozen nuclear power plants to levy the burden on relying on western fossil fuel. The nuclear energy divergent was merely a guise for the production of nuclear weaponry. These armaments were produced, stockpiled and sold to SA's eastern allies.

South Africa's coastal peak was converted as a strategic point for shipping trade routes from Asia to Europe that did not move through a war zone. Eventually it was bombarded when the SA navy left to fight another country's war, exposing the coast to ghost bombings of drones that came on submarines. The bombings crippled the South African military and gave the rebellion just enough footing to topple the government. But when the regime was overthrown, the threat of the nuclear weapons fell into the hands of the native/ rebels who refused any international co-operation. Every nation was anxious, the situation was dire now that these destructive chariots of the Armageddon were in the hands of those not easily swayed by money, and didn't have the best interest of the 1% at heart. Who knows what they might do? Apparently there was only one solution to the problem. Chaos it seems is contagious. And so because of fear, a torrent of nuclear warheads added to the chaos which resulted in 50 million Hardworking South Africans losing their lives in what was supposed to be a fair democratic society. In 2033 South Africa was destroyed. Every major city was laid to waste and most coastline towns were eradicated. The cradle of life became the cradle of death. A thumbprint in the desert sand... Seemingly over-night modern society was relegated to dust, their homes, histories, cultures all wiped off the face of the earth in thunderous glory. And like Marikana, all that was left of the people were etches in stone, their shadows burnt into the walls at the moment of their evaporation.

It is not clear who was responsible as there are many theories, ranging from the Americans, to the Russians, to self-detonations, to aliens even. Peace always has a toll that must be paid every now and then and since the start of the industrial age, that toll has become an incrementally burden.

The skies ignited into an unending fire storm and began corroding the atmosphere. A dragon's rage of a flame that engulfed all that was left. Scores of fire that were so hot they melted concrete boiled up water sources, evaporating it into a fleeting steam. The fires were not raging but burned with a methodical, consistent aspect. What remained of the cities were now being eaten by flames that birthed up into the sky choking black smoke, buildings looked like dying candles on a windowsill. The sky was gone, hidden above a blanket of ash so that no light from Sol could shine through. Instead the only caressing light was from the hungry flames that coated everything in a flickering amber glow and made shadows dance in jaggedly-jazzy mimes. As time went by the fires congregated into a monolithic looming mountain of a flame, a blaze, that started creating its own weather, inhaling gulps of air and everything else as if the heart of this flame housed a vacuuming black hole. In the ancient Greek myth the titan Prometheus took pity on humans. He stole fire from the gods and gave it to them. In the myth the fire represented knowledge. Then this mountain of flame was the gross mutation of this gift, a testament to its misuse and danger of knowledge. The gods were right to withhold it from us.

The earth had been returned to some chaotic primordial state like in the beginning of time, like God was creating the world; un-creating the world.

Without sunlight, the Phytoplankton in the sea began dying out. These plants were essential for animal life to thrive and shortly after their dispersion, the ocean stopped beating. Fish began to wash up on irradiated shores. Migratory birds started falling out of the sky and dying in the millions. The upside was that at least for a while there would be food. The land was drenched in darkness and the dying. The veil of ash in certain parts blocked out the sun for almost half a decade! South Africa was transformed into a fiery alien landscape peppered with titanic dimples and graveyards of rubble. The worst was yet to come. The earth was still in its last death throws and someone had to pay. The sin of the father would become the sin of the son and whoever was left surviving would know the true definition of hell.

After years of living in the purgatory of post bombed SA a phase began known as the passing. Things began to stabilize enough for changes to be apparent. And things were indeed different, changed beyond imagination, beyond recognition.

The great flame was dying out and the sky was clearing up. The ashy clouds, urged on by the wind, moved to greener pastures to rain their choking cargo down upon. We see those black snowflakes in the winter season instead of rain. The fleeing ash clouds, like stage curtains revealed the beloved Sol once again. It was a most glorious, most praised moment but the heats from its warm rays were different, sharper even, more concentrated. Things became hotter and days became longer. And any extended stay in sun drenched areas would render you mad. The sun was apathetic to the cause of life. Or maybe it always was.

With the coming of the new season came new challenges. The earth became murky like some step brother of Venus.

Fierce but concentrated storms with scimitar winds began slashing up irregularly, bringing with them poisonous rain. The weather it seems began taking on schizophrenic mind-set although still seemed deliberate on occasions. These cold storms, as they were dubbed, are seen as bad omens. If you are caught in one, death is certain. So always check the horizon before choosing to venture. The earth also began shaking as if in constant bombardment, however, it was internal shuffling. Tectonic earthquakes would crack open and the hungry earth would swallow the land leaving in its wake gaping cliffs that fell into"nowhere-ness" and nothing. The world it seemed was as hungry as its starving survivors. Not only was the earth starving but it was thirsty. Water was difficult to come by and meticulously controlled. Even before the attack, water was an issue and under regulation. But now it was a commodity. An unopened bottle of water was gold, liquid gold. And if people were murderers for their wealth in gold, they become demons for a drink of water. The nuclear weapons left an irradiated legacy, contaminating the soil and the atmosphere, transforming the physics of the land into unimaginable prospects. The only place you could go to escape the radiation was underground, to which many people fled. The radiation would melt you before you could realize it. Their invisible spectrums were littered across the land like the ghost of those that have died. And nothing managed to escape their taint. Most of the water is unsanitary. Almost all the food save for those in deep freezers. Along with gravity and magnetism, radiation would be the next constant. And no baby born would ever be completely human again. This was the new age of man, the age of the nuclear man.

Not all was at a loss, the destruction of what was known as

South Africa gave birth to a new land now called New Azania. And all people could bring with to this new land was their memories. Their dreams they had to bury along with the ashes of their loved ones. The only thing that managed to survive was the fynbos. This is no surprise because fynbos are used to living in harsh environments and use fire to restart their life cycles, the phoenix of the vegetation ecosystems. If only people were as resilient as the fynbos.

All water is holy.
A cosmic gift of perfection...

THE CULT OF OSIRIS

(Sons of Osiris)

Long ago a mysterious cult Rose to power, gathered followers and waged war to reclaim Africa. A cult based on sacrifice. Rumours surfaced about them sacrificing people and even children. The people merely let this happen which is why they say the ancestors punished Africa with the great storm. Like what God did to Sodom and Gomorra, our African Eden was razed to the ground once more.

The moral ineptitude of past African leaders has opened up the door and set the stage for people to yearn for a more moral, forward looking leadership that would offer them spiritual appeasement while imbuing them with pride to be the sons and daughters of Africa, of Osiris. People were done with the corruptible, human politicians who over the course of the years have been shown to be all too human. They needed a deity, or at least a figure close enough to be a deity. The sons of Osiris were not just one person or one leader, they were a council of leaders that all vowed to serve the land of Africa to appease their god of the underworld, lord of the living ones, who wished his people a prosperous existence. That was their only goal. And they were sincere about the revival of African spirituality but at a great cost. Osiris is the Egyptian god of the dead but the cult did not worship him by traditional means. The way they would honour their deity is by behaving like him and carrying out his will. Osiris was associated with death and rebirth, so too the cult wished destruction and rebirth to fall upon their beloved Eden which has been corrupted by western ideals. The Sons of Osiris set their sights on reclaiming Africa. Many a people stood behind them and they garnered followers as well as fanatics. For once Africans were waking up and becoming spiritually free. They had a meaningful purpose. The Osiris reform brought prosperity and with existing international ties with the Russians and Chinese they were capable of launching a full-scale reclamation campaign. At the time, the environment had become very hot and arid and the central strategy of the campaign became the fight and control for water, and with this water they were able to leverage allegiance. South Africa became more advanced with every military victory attained. Eventually the Southern tip of Africa was renamed New Azania and to the Sons of Osiris it was aptly named the cradle of gold. For they held nothing in more accord then the warm embrace of the golden hue. The wars claimed many lives and in order to ensure the soldiers safe travel to the underworld, ceremonial sacrifices were held. The head of these sacrificial war monks were called the order of Owls. They donned Owl vestments and spilled blood in the name of war. Things were definitely getting topsy-turvy. The logic and peace fought for by previous generations were discarded by immoral snakes. But it was too late, the age of industrialization had left people empty and depersonalized. What the Sons of Osiris offered was divinity, a chance to start anew. However, the path to divinity had trickles of blood leading up to the severed head of the old world values. And so rebellion broke out. Chaos slowly filled the land and people's minds. Things were not the same anymore. Things were unfair. A fighting spirit was born to regain the peace they once enjoyed but the peace never came. Terrorism reigned, chaos reigned, and war reigned. All while society broke down and fell... Communication fell. The togetherness and community and universality of human connection ceased to be.

While fighting to unite Africa under the New Azanian flag, war was breaking out in the homeland. And so to quell the rebellious upheaval, water was put under heavy regulation and safe guard. People were reformed by the necessity for the life giving liquid. And so once again peace came over the land and the pagan traditions continued, got worse. More sacrifices were being made in the name of the god of the dead and afterlife. These sacrificial ceremonies were festivals of blood that entranced people with jigs and jives of lunacy and regressed man into animalistic pack like beasts that cry for slaughter. They celebrated death and in doing so never felt more alive. It was the height of African civilization, New Azania the cradle of gold.

Osiris, god of death and afterlife had
a rival in his brother Seth
who was aptly the god of storms...

HISTORY UNTOLD

The nature of the degradation of human civilization into a new yet primal form is due to a number of independent but interrelated circumstances. One main factor is the lack of fossil fuels which brought in the second nuclear age and with it, the fear of nuclear power in relation to the environment. Fossil fuel began degrading at an exorbitant rate. Some say it is related to the spike in population. Power consumption was at an all-time high and to compensate South Africa had previously signed a nuclear power deal with Russia which brokered in many nuclear power plants around the cape. However, the issue of nuclear waste disposal was always a problem. So they stored it underground. The nuclear waste began contaminating the soil and things stopped growing. Meanwhile war was in full throttle in African countries surrounding New Azania isolating the African pinnacle between its two oceans. The deals with the Russians and Chinese had given N.A heavy military capitol and when the conflict in Europe started they were drawn in as well. Peace lasted for a while, but to usher in the new age of idealism, blood had to be levied.

The battle of this age was to root out antiquated western industrialist ideals from Africa. Their economies were dying and so were their fighting capacity. So, with the Chinese and Russian allies, New Azania launched a campaign to unite lower Southern Africa under one flag. Together with Zimbabwe, Botswana and Namibia. The campaign was the biggest military project launched on African soil. With New Azania's significant nuclear prowess, they started developing nuclear weapons at an alarming rate. And seemingly overnight they became a sleeper super power. Western corporations started being bought up by singular entities and overthrew governments. One of these entities was the corporation LAS which was heavily involved in the Namibian crisis war 2020. The ideal of democracy was waning thin and capitalism was dehumanizing people into currency rather than individuals. It became clear that new era of idealism was necessary which is why the Sons of Osiris or S.O had so much support, nationally and internationally. The wars were showing to be a benefit to N.A's economy, population issue and unemployment issue. Anyone could take up arms and fight for the motherland, with Russian weapons and Chinese made vehicles. Despite these international influences New Azanian leaders never lost sight of their heritage. They still kept the quick buck in mind and quickly became obsessed with stockpiling, gold, iridium and water. Western mega business was not about to allow Africa to obtain its supposed independence from their lecherous vines and so began funding a top-secret project in order to hold them at ransom. A show of power... They say that life started in Africa. Well it's only fitting that it should start dying from there as well.

Friday 17, April 2029 New Azanian coastal territories were hit with a storm of epic proportion. Overnight, major provinces were razed by violent winds and some records show, actual fire hailing from the sky. Places became heavily flooded and water sources became diseased due to the deceased infecting pools of drinkable water. The disaster had displaced so many people that emergency areas became grossly overpopulated. A new disease broke out, in a form of pox that infects and inflames the brain. Symptoms were measles on the pupils and around the eyes. Eventually civil war broke out. Handfuls of people were trying to fight over the scarce remaining resources. Soon the Sons of Osiris were overthrown but instead of another government taking over, a generic feudal system was implemented where people, who could fight, like those who were soldiers by trade, would protect those who were not, like farmers, craftsman and Doctors, in exchange for their services. Parts of land were allocated to the lords or chieftains to govern and protect, leading small communities to be built in and around these lands. Eventually this system fell apart when chieftains tried to take land from one another. It is ironic because the land wasn't worth anything. The soil degradation had rendered it inhabitable. Basically they were just fighting for the sake of it. Soon the landscapes became frequent victims of weather abuse. But something about these storms were different. If caught outside, there was a high chance of you being killed. Earthquakes became frequent, ripping great chasms into the once stable land. Some say that these chasms attract evil spirits. These earthquakes were chopping and changing the landscape and laying mountains to dust. It's as if the land was cursed, maybe we never appeased the ancestors enough. Nuclear power plants were destroyed which released their radioactive cargo and added further to the environmental issues and slowly but surely the land was greatly poisoned and became a scarred barren wasteland with festering sores and pockets of radiation. The radiation got swept up into the atmosphere and worsened the weather. There was this constant exposure to radiation and the only way to escape it was to die. The earth heated up immensely as if there was nothing diluting the sun's rays giving rise to an ailment they would come to call heat sickness. The ice caps were melting and raised the sea levels bringing in the coast as well as stringing new rivers through the land. But this water was exceptionally tainted by salt water parasites. Drinking a handful would infect you with more than a hundred teething worms that could each grow up to a kilogram in size. The feudal/ tribal system had failed to keep peace but some groups still survived by forging straight ahead into the fray of madness. Eventually the rest of the world was cut off. They were not a concern for the people of New Cape who were occupied largely with the day to day hell. In fact it did not actually matter. To them No other place existed.

Just as society changed, the earth was changing. A tumultuous metamorphosis that shredded through whatever life was in the way. Some speculate that the monstrous storm of 2027 was due to a super weapon, other say it's because of a satellite slow heating the ocean, changing ocean currents and the weather. Others say it's the wrath of god. It never took long for civilization to break down afterward. Hope had been squandered. There was nothing to rebuild or to return to. Lack of national structure meant that basic needs were not a provided for. Some built and some destroyed and unfortunately the ones who built were too busy building and got destroyed. And so nothing managed to rise up from the ashes, for war is human nature. Homo-sapiens are nothing if not an anagram for adaptable, no matter how disheartening or horrific the circumstance. But this time, this time was different. The adjustment was too steep and many were weaned out. There is no space age, there is no information revolution. No high understanding, no universal health care. No utopia. Since antiquity civilization builds itself up to great heights and then destroys itself. Like Atlantis, Rome and USA. Africa has been built and destroyed many times. But god might have finally abandoned us it. It's like everywhere you go all you see are memories.

Things people used to think were important. We have been made humble. The flame of Prometheus has engulfed the world and burnt it to ashes. And we are forced to rise, not newly formed from ashes like the phoenix, but with burn wounds that have incinerated our nerves until we are unable to feel.

"I think therefore I am",
has been replaced with
"I live therefore I am."

It really is a most defining
era of mankind where the
strong truly survive.

WHAT THE WORLD TURNED INTO

a genuine account

Eventually everything distilled into suburban dust towns filled with wasted dreams and echoes of insatiable greed and incoherent wants. Everything just seems so empty. A constant wind blowing over your tracks makes it impossible to determine which way you came from. The land is mired with conflict. Groups or tribes are at constant war with one another. A war for sport and fun... A way to pass the time but also a war for survival and supplies... Life is a desperate struggle. The people are scattered across the wounded land enduring each day. If sickness hits, that's it, you're dead. You have to ensure that you are always armed and ready to fight because you never know what horror awaits you around that corner. Cities are haunted husks, housing demonic whispers of anguish while the wilderness is home to unfathomable mutations that will make you tear your eyes out. Water is scarce, it always has been. If there's a man standing between you and a pint of the blue stuff make sure to kill him first otherwise it's going to be your head hitting the dirt. You can't trust anyone, ever, naiveté gets you killed. The sooner you learn that everyone is out for themselves, the easier it will be to kill, the easier you'll sleep. Survival is a one man game, if someone else is taking the spoils chances are you shit out of luck and die. You could band together, join the frontier, a militia group based in the cape, they focus on usurping territory from the savages and securing trade routes and mainly deal with trade and transportation of water. When joining up they'll tell you it's for a good cause but despite the bullshit, they feed and arm you, and you will never meet a more hardy band of wet trigger killers except for the owls they'll slit your throat before you can plead for help. They can't be reasoned with, unless you are one of them or have liquid currency, so stay out of the mountains. Life is uncertain, so instead of sitting in one place waiting to get ambushed, people usually travel around from place to place. Growing conflict has made certain area off limits, unless you want to get your hands on some of the action. But be warned, stepping out into the field on a trek will take every ounce of you. The elements are not your friends. The sun will fry you. If it doesn't it will cook you brains to mush and you will be sucking sand until you die or until some jackals eat you. Its best you travel at night, when it's cooler. The moon is slightly more forgiving. However, night time offers its own set of unique challenges. When travelling at night it is very important you make as little noise as possible because there are things that roost in the dark. Bad things. I've seen a man ripped in half while he was sleeping. He was dead before he even realized it. You should also watch out for pockets of radiation. A long time ago they buried something in the earth and it poisoned the land. So when you see the ground bubbling, chances are it's' too late for you. Prepare to have your skin melted off your bones. Water is currency out here. If you find some bottled or untainted water, don't tell anybody. You just bought yourself a couple more days on this hot hell. Don't ever drink the water you find on the ground, its radiation affected or worse, parasites. One sip and it's a done deal for you. But the thirst is a demon to fight off. The dryness will overthrow any logical thought. That's why it's important for you to have an exit strategy, when you know your fate is sealed then you should just off yourself. Otherwise you might get desperate and drink from some tainted mud hole. Next thing you know you playing host to thousands of wormy tenants attaching themselves to your spine. It's not so bad, I heard about a scrap Berge who spoke to his worm like it was a person. The bastard is still going strong. Watch out for mine fields. They were planted a long time ago on main roads and such but are still very active. Also if you manage to deactivate one of them I know a guy in trade city who will buy it from you. Just ask for Bonsai. There is not much ways to get around besides using your foette-bikes. You could take a motor to get around but most don't work, the electronics are fried. People mostly live in them now. The Glazers run the train track, they have a deal with the frontier as a transport route but mostly the Glazers use it to pillage anyone along their route and use the train as a fast getaway. If you hear those metallic skids, hide your ass away. The glazers are adept archers and have a taste for indigenous meat. Food is hard to come by as well, that is if you don't eat man-meat. Shit don't grow anymore and what does grow gets burnt up by the sun. Out here you have to train yourself to forget the taste of food. That way, you don't get as hungry. Things are also a bit different. You'll notice immediately that no watches work. So it's impossible to know the time. All you can be sure of is that the sun will set eventually. It's harsh out there. You have to keep your guard up and come to terms that it is never safe. But recently I'm starting to realize that it's not the worldly things I should be afraid of. There are things out there, in the shadows of those broken buildings that I don't trust. Nothing is that calm and quiet. I can't help but feel like it is a trap. I never pass through buildings if I can help it. Out there, anything can happen. You can't be prepared for all of them, so be prepared to die.

But one thing you should never
do is go down without a fight.